Blood Curdling Ballots

A Paranormal Cozy Mystery Short Read

B I Skinner

Contents

1. Chapter 1   1

2. Chapter 2   12

3. Chapter 3   18

4. Chapter 4   22

5. Chapter 5   28

6. Chapter 6   30

7. Chapter 7   35

8. Chapter 8   41

9. Chapter 9   46

10. Chapter 10   51

11. Chapter 11   56

12. Chapter 12   63

13. Chapter 13   69

14. Chapter 14   75

15. Chapter 15   80

16. Chapter 16   88

17. Chapter 17   96

18.   Chapter 18   102

More Books by B I Skinner   105

Copyright   108

Chapter 1

"Trick or treat!" a large group of children shout so loudly it startles me.

Adding to the din, Marshall and Marcus, my rabbit familiars, keep turning up the stereo that's playing spooky Halloween music.

"For the last time, you two, turn it down!" I scold them.

Yes, that's right. The *rabbits*. My rabbit familiars. Or rather, my Gran's rabbit familiars, that I inherited when she died. Her magical ability to communicate with them also transferred to me, although I can't explain why.

It's Halloween night, and we've decked out Marcall's Vegetarian Breakfast Cafe - also inherited from Gran - like never before. Halloween is extra special this year because I'm running for Crested Peaks Mayor, with the election only a week away.

Last year's Halloween Festival was celebrated at the Hotel Glacier where the town mortician dropped dead from poisoning in front of the entire ballroom.

Thankfully, aside from the election bickering, this year has been quiet so far. I'm desperately hoping it stays that way. What are the odds of finding a dead body on Halloween night two years in a row?

Then, on top of everything else that's happening this evening, I'm debating my mayoral opponent in the Crested Peaks Cemetery at midnight. I don't know why the City Council thought that was a good idea. Who wants to watch us debate on Halloween in a graveyard?

I'm trying to review my debate notes, but it's so loud and chaotic I'm not getting very far. This is my second set of notes, by the way, because the rabbits ate the first set. I swear it's their life's mission to cause trouble.

My Gran always claimed she won them in a poker game decades ago, which makes me question how old they must be, but they refuse to tell me. They're super cute - don't tell them I said that - with their ginger-colored spots and crooked helicopter ears.

Even I must admit, although they frequently drive me crazy, they're very good at helping me solve the murders that pop up in Crested Peaks at the most unfortunate times.

They like to wander the town pestering shop keepers for treats, so everyone in Crested Peaks knows who they are, and they often overhear conversations and see things that the police don't.

I also can't forget that Gran named Marcall's, the cafe, after them by combining their names. This was long before it became a celebrity thing. She always claimed she invented that. Who knows, maybe she did!

Stumpy, the two-footed cat, and their best friend came later. Before Serenity's Sweets candy shop moved in next door, it was an Italian restaurant where Stumpy lived. After the owner met an unfortunate end, the new owner, Alice, of Alice's Tavern, kicked him out.

Then Marshall and Marcus invited him to live with us. Without telling me. He followed us out to my car after closing one night, and that's when they explained he was coming home with us.

His back legs are stumps, but you'd be surprised how well he gets around on his front feet. He told Marshall and Marcus that he's a war veteran. I'm not sure how that's possible, yet I now have three talking animals living with me. So I guess anything is possible.

"Relax, boss, you'll do great," Damien, Marcall's supremely talented chef, tells me, giving me a quick shoulder massage. He worked for my Gran before she passed and is one of the reasons I decided to keep the cafe after he agreed to stay on.

We wouldn't be the success we are today without him. His Damien Special, a massive breakfast burrito full of eggs, black beans, cheese, potatoes, grilled jalapenos, and caramelized onions, along with a secret sauce he refuses to reveal even to me, draws in tourists from everywhere. We have to be well stocked in the winter because large groups of skiers flock here on their way to the slopes.

He's a short, stocky Cuban immigrant whose family moved to the US when he was a little boy. *He* prefers the term height-challenged. I just tell him he's short. I'm 5 feet 10 though, so to me, a lot of people are short. His Cuban background and secret family recipes are the basis for many of the dishes he creates for Marcall's.

"Yuck. I still don't see why we're doing this at midnight in the graveyard," I lament.

"Don't worry about it. You'll wipe the floor with this guy. Our internal polling has you way ahead."

"You chasing after 47 people at the grocery store, asking them how they plan to vote doesn't constitute a poll," I remind him.

"Aw, c'mon, lighten up. It will be fun!" he says, wiggling his fingers, making what he considers ghost noises. We have ghosts in Crested Peaks - the most famous one is Harvey, who works at the Hotel Glacier - but I don't think any of them sound like that.

Marcall's is a breakfast cafe, so we aren't typically open at night, which has Damien eager to prepare festive Halloween snacks, like fried pumpkin ravioli with a side of brown butter sauce for dipping. Kids get a personal pizza with ghosts made from mozzarella and olives.

Of course, we can't forget our famous cinnamon and sugar low-calorie donuts (that taste exactly like regular donuts) made from Damien's exclusive recipe and a bit of my witchcraft. It's a recipe that's literally worth killing for, as Damien learned the hard way last year!

I suggested we add pumpkin pie martinis, but everyone insisted that should be *after* the debate. When I argue it would make the debate much more interesting, they ignore me.

I had to settle for hot - non spiked - cider instead. I made it myself using one of my Gran's special brews. While it isn't the same as a pumpkin pie martini, it's still delicious.

"Trick or treat!" a tiny unicorn bellows as she bursts through the door. It's Poppy (although in this town, you never know), Damien and Tom's adopted foster daughter.

She can barely walk in the elaborate costume, but she doesn't care. She proudly holds up her plastic pumpkin bucket with flashing orange lights. "You're supposed to put candy in here!" she informs me.

"You don't say!" I laugh.

Damien and Tom were shocked when we told them Poppy is a witch. It was no surprise to me, of course. Marshall and Marcus also noticed it right away. What I can't explain is how Poppy is able to communicate with Marshall, Marcus, *and* Stumpy. Not even I can talk to Stumpy. We have no idea why; we just go with it.

"Charlotte! Guess what?" she shouts.

"What?" I shout back.

"I get to stay up until midnight for your debate!"

She's so excited I hate to burst her bubble.

"Do you know what a debate is?"

"No!" she squeals with laughter.

Tom sets her up at a table with a cup of hot cider - an ice cube added to cool it down - and a pizza.

"Happy Halloween, everyone!" Serenity from Serenity's Sweets Candy Shop next door to Marcall's announces as she hurries through the door. She has a tray of the most mouthwatering, gorgeous, candied apples I've ever seen. "A special present just for my next-door neighbors," she tells us.

She's placed an array of dazzling apples on a silver tray. They're covered in red, caramel, black, and purple. How did she make black candied apples, I wonder? Each shiny silver skewer has a crisp orange bow tied around it. I can't stop staring at them.

The purple candied apples are so shiny I can see myself in them. The caramel apples are dipped in nuts and colorful sprinkles. Each one is like a little piece of artwork. I want to ask her how she did this, but who am I kidding? Like I'd ever be able to replicate it, anyway. I guess I don't need to, considering she's just next door.

"How will we ever eat those?" I ask. "They're too pretty!"

"I'm sure you'll find a way," she laughs.

The minute Poppy sees them, she abandons her pizza. "Those are for after dinner!" Tom reminds her as Damien hurries into the back with the tray before she can get any more ideas. I don't know how they do it sometimes. Parenting must be so hard.

"Hide those from the rabbits, too!" I shout at him. Like I said, parenting must be hard.

Serenity's Sweets moved in next door last winter after a laborious search by Rita, the landlord. The previous tenants didn't work out exactly as she'd hoped, so she was extra careful with Serenity, for which I'm incredibly grateful. Considering the previous tenants didn't work out as *I* had expected either!

Serenity reminds me of Gran, and I often seek her advice. She's not just a witch like Gran was; she's level-headed, patient, and wise also like Gran. I also love that she looks like someone who could play Mrs. Claus in a Christmas movie with her silver hair and well-padded frame.

Who would trust a skinny candy maker? Her shop is exactly how you'd picture a candy store run by a witch, with enchanted sweets and decorations throughout. Stumpy thinks her shop smells of "sugar and spice and everything nice."

"All set for the big debate, kiddo?" she asks.

I grimace. "Any chance you could whip up some kind of town emergency, so they cancel the debate?" I respond.

"Bite your tongue!" she scolds. "Don't you dare put that kind of energy out there."

"Sorry," I sigh. "You're right. I take it back. I can't wait for the debate to start!"

She narrows her eyes at me. "I don't know why you're so nervous. I've seen you poring over those notes all week. You'll do great!"

"I keep telling her the same thing!" Aranya exclaims, throwing her arm around me and squeezing me tight.

Discovering Aranya was a lucky accident. Once the cafe got busy enough, Damien and I knew we needed extra help, so we didn't have to be here every second of the day. I met her one evening at the Crested Peaks Farmers Market while ordering from her parents' Thai One On food truck.

She already knew Marshall, Marcus, and Stumpy because they often visit the truck hoping for treats. Cilantro for the rabbits and chicken for Stumpy, of course. She's a culinary student at Colorado Mountain College and was looking for part-time work in a restaurant. One that didn't belong to her parents, that is.

Last summer, we were shocked when her father was accused of murdering the former mayor after they got into a fistfight at the 4th of July Festival. The mayor had sharply increased rent prices on the food truck lot that he just happened to own. Tensions were high.

After increasing the prices so much that many of the food truck owners couldn't afford it, he took the additional step of banning the trucks from parking on the street. When I realized these types of shenanigans were just the tip of the iceberg, I shocked everyone, including myself, by throwing my hat in the ring for mayor.

I've promised the voters that, if elected mayor, I'll prohibit the types of unethical behavior we've witnessed recently from this town's elected officials. Unsurprisingly, a few of the previous Mayor's old friends, who are still on the City Council, vehemently oppose this. But I have heard from so many Crested Peaks residents who enthusiastically support cleaning up the city council that I'm inspired to keep pressing for reform.

"You know that you and your parents' support have meant the world to me!" I tell her.

"Boss, if it weren't for you, my dad might be in jail for murder," she reminds me.

"Nah," I dismiss it with a wave of my hand. "Everyone knew your dad was innocent."

"We need you to win next week so we can throw the bums out!" as my dad says.

"I'll do my best!" I assure her.

"My parents are meeting us at the debate tonight!" she tells me.

I cringe. "Tell your parents they really don't need to come. It's midnight, after all."

"But they wouldn't miss it! They're your biggest fans," she insists.

"They can't be her biggest fans because we are!" My best friend and witching mentor Miranda announces as she and her boyfriend Miles, the town librarian, make their way through the growing crowd of people in the cafe.

I've known Miranda since high school, but we only reconnected when I moved back. She owns the coffee shop across the street from Marcall's called Bean Around a Bit.

Another one of my short friends, she's just a smidge taller than Damien. Tonight, her short spiky hair, with color she changes in an instant to match her mood or, in this case, the holiday, is bright orange with purple streaks throughout.

Changing hair color was one of the first tricks she taught me when I moved back, and I think it's one of the best parts about being a witch. It's an incredibly useful spell that lets me change hair color by the day or even just to match my outfit.

I left Crested Peaks the second I graduated from high school, never planning to return. I'd had enough of this town. My mom was a witch, my dad a wizard, or *Supernaturals* as they call us, were also con artists who were murdered by another thief in an illegal scheme gone wrong.

I convinced myself that if I moved as far away as possible, Manhattan to be precise, and refused to admit, even to myself, that I was a witch, life would be great. By denying my supernatural abilities, I was confident I wouldn't become a crook like my parents. You've probably already guessed how well that turned out.

Everything went fine for a while. I was even engaged to be married. Then my fiancé broke up with me to star in a reality tv show. The next day I got fired from my job when I transferred a call to my boss but mixed up his wife with his girlfriend. How was I supposed to keep these things straight?

Then my Gran died. She left me the cafe, her house, and her rabbits so I came back, but after years of denying my supernatural abilities, I was sorely lacking in the witching department. Miranda has helped me a ton with that. Gran never pushed me to use magic. I think somehow, she knew that I'd learn when I was ready.

I didn't want to take on her business at first either. I planned to sell everything and run. But the first time I walked into the cafe, after she had passed, I sensed her presence, and I knew that I should carry on her legacy for her sake. It comforted me to think of how pleased she would be.

Eventually, however, it became something I wanted to do for myself. I wanted a successful breakfast cafe for me and knowing that I was carrying on my grandma's legacy was just a bonus. Now here I am, running for Crested Peaks mayor. Can you believe that? I certainly can't.

"Listen up everybody! It's almost time!" Detective Andrew Bailey of the Crested Peaks Police Department announces. "We're heading to the cemetery!"

I met Detective Bailey, or Drew, as I call him when we were in high school. We kissed. Then he ghosted me. No, not literally, even though this is Crested Peaks. He just stopped speaking to me.

Naturally, teenage me assumed I was the worst kisser ever. Fast forward ten years later when we meet again over a dead body in an alley. I was shocked to learn he was a cop and a detective even. The dead guy was Marcall's landlord, and I was the primary suspect for a while.

I eventually found out that he ghosted me in high school because his friends and family were furious when they realized he was spending time with the town pariah. The girl from the other side of the tracks. The one from *that* family. His family forbade him from seeing me.

But after I figured out who really murdered my landlord, no, it wasn't me; we started dating. We butt heads regularly due to my tendency to get overly involved in police matters. Can I help if my familiars have a knack for finding dead people?

Have I mentioned how handsome he is? Ridiculously good-looking, if you ask me. He fits the very definition of tall, dark, and handsome. Over six feet tall with short dark hair, a chiseled jawline, and deep emerald eyes.

Gladys, one of our cafe regulars, is always flirting with him. Which, considering she's old enough to be his grandma, is extra amusing. She was disappointed when he made detective only because he stopped wearing his beat cop uniform.

Now here I am on Halloween night preparing to debate the opposition. My opponent, Herbert Appleton, hasn't been the most, uh, agreeable person to put it politely. He's made numerous personal jabs about my being a witch. He even brought up the stories about my crooked parents, which fell flat because it's old news to everyone in Crested Peaks, anyway.

The only time I really lost my temper with him, though, was when he pointed out how weird it is that my rabbit familiars and Stumpy follow me everywhere. Then he made a most ungracious comment about what he would do with rabbits if they followed *him* around.

Fortunately, Drew was there and knew what was coming. Just as I lunged for Herb, preparing to slap him into next week, Drew grabbed me and pulled me aside. Of course, several people filmed it on camera, so it ended up on the internet.

It was kind of embarrassing. The clip went viral, and some clever souls produced astonishingly creative memes out of it. A lot of people told me afterwards they were surprised it took me that long. They claimed *they* would have done it long before that. Tradition dictates

I should have apologized, but I didn't. Call *me* whatever names you want, but when you threaten the rabbits, all bets are off.

After that, he claimed I was violent, so he hired bodyguards to protect himself. I never knew politics could be so theatrical.

Now that Drew has announced it's almost midnight, everyone in the cafe gathers to form a parade. The rabbits and Stumpy ride in a wagon I often use to cart them around town while Bubbles, Damien, and Tom's black and white pitty-mix walks beside it.

She's wearing a Crested Peaks Chooses Charlotte t-shirt. Unlike Marshall, Marcus, and Stumpy, she doesn't talk. Marshall and Marcus think this is weird. Animals that don't talk are unnatural, they tell me.

Everyone is wearing the enchanted campaign buttons Miranda made. They're super clever, designed to look like a movie marquee where the lights around the edge of the button flash and the letters inside sparkle.

In one of his many personal digs, my opponent pointed out that the buttons are witchcraft. Miranda was worried voters would hold it against me, but I told her to ignore him. Then I insisted she make as many enchanted buttons as she could.

The atmosphere is electric, and everyone is excited. I wish I could be too. I hate being such a debbie downer, but I really don't want to do this debate. I feel like we're laughing at fate hosting a debate on Halloween in a graveyard. What if we're asking for trouble?

Chapter 2

When we arrive at the graveyard, the people in charge of the event show us where to go. They point out which podium is mine, and the other is for my opponent. The moderators, who will ask the questions and keep track of the time, introduce themselves.

I hope my hands aren't as sweaty as I fear when I shake hands with them. Drew gives me a quick kiss for good luck before taking his seat in the audience.

The whispering starts at 10 minutes after midnight when my opponent still hasn't shown up. Did he chicken out? Drink too much pumpkin beer? Does he know where he's supposed to be? Like this wasn't already nerve-wracking, now I must endure the uncomfortable stares of being the only one up here.

When Marshall, Marcus, and Stumpy jump out of the wagon and wander into the graveyard, I want to shout at them to stay close, but then people will question my sanity.

Everyone in town knows I'm a witch, but few know about Marshall, Marcus, and Stumpy. First, who would even believe me? Second, if they did, believe me, I worry that they could try to exploit their talents, or worse yet, they could try to harm them.

I shudder just thinking about it. It has presented some challenges when people wonder about the dead bodies or catch me talking to them.

They return several minutes later just as the organizers are about to cancel the debate, I watch the animals hurry straight for me. Uh oh. This can't be good.

"Hey, lady! Guess what?" Marcus shouts.

Oh no, no, no, no, not again. It always starts with them shouting *hey, lady!*

"We found your opponent!" Marshall announces.

"Where?" I sigh as people nearby twist around to see who I'm talking to. "C'mon! We'll show you," Marcus tells me.

Why me?

"Excuse me," I tell the announcer. "I'll be right back."

He's confused, but at this point, no one really thinks Herb will show up, anyway. I follow the boys, praying they're mistaken. Just this one time, can't they be wrong? Can't it be a Halloween decoration? Or someone passed out drunk?

The boys zigzag through the headstones as thick fog rolls in. I shiver at the chill in the air, I didn't notice before. That's appropriate, isn't it? In the distance, a coyote howls.

When I realize a small crowd is now following us, I try to shoo them away, to no avail. Even though Marcus, Marshall, and Stumpy are leading the way, as far as the crowd knows, I'm the one who knows where I'm going.

We finally arrive at the body; sure enough, it's Herb Appleton. With a hatchet sticking out of his back. Weirdly, it looks an awful lot like mine. The one I use to cut apple branches for the rabbits to chew on. Although I imagine they all look alike.

I bend over him to get a closer look. I'm so disturbed about seeing yet another dead body that I've forgotten the crowd of people following us until someone screams.

That sets off a chain reaction as more gather around to see what the fuss is. Once they realize it's a body, they scream too. Drew breaks through the crowd. When he sees the body, he sighs heavily. "Not again!"

Marshall, Marcus, and Stumpy stare at me like we told you so.

"How do they do this?" Drew hisses.

"Believe me, if I knew, I'd stop it!" I hiss back.

Drew goes into detective mode, calling for backup and the Medical Examiner's Office while barking at the crowd to back up and not touch anything. Whispers roll through the group while people stare at me, point fingers, and shake their heads.

"What does this mean?" Drew asks.

"He was murdered?" I respond in confusion. What does he mean, what does this mean? He's the detective, isn't he?

"What does this mean for the mayoral race? Your opponent is dead!"

Uh oh. That didn't even cross my mind yet. "I have no idea what happens next."

"Ms. Duffin! Ms. Duffin! Polly Hughes, reporter for Mountain News! Did you murder your opponent?"

"What? No! No, I didn't murder my opponent! What's wrong with you?" I take a step toward him, scaring him so much that he backs up.

"Char," Drew warns with a hand on my arm. "You're on camera," he says under his breath.

I pause while the crowd's murmuring intensifies. I didn't just inherit my supernatural gifts from my parents; I'm afraid I got their tempers too.

More officers from the CPPD arrive along with the Medical Examiner. They place yellow tape around the crime scene while pulling me aside to ask me how I knew where the body was. Gee, officer, I just followed my talking rabbits. They have a habit of finding bodies, you know.

"I went for a walk to focus while waiting for the debate to start."

"You walk through a graveyard at midnight on Halloween to get focused?" the officer asks.

"Well, to be fair, I was already here. I was waiting for my opponent," I remind him, pointing at my now dead opponent.

"One of the witnesses says it looked like you knew right where to go," he informs me.

I pinch my lips together but then remind myself to smile because everyone is watching. "They're mistaken," I tell him through clenched teeth.

Eventually, everyone is pushed back as Drew and the rest of the CPPD block off the area to investigate the scene.

"Excuse me! Charlotte! Jack Scott, from the Crested Peaks Times, any idea how this could have happened?"

"How would I know that?" I scowl at her.

"Well, he is, uh, was your opponent in the mayoral race, and you were seen arguing several times in the last few weeks."

"That's no reason to kill him!" I snap.

"Didn't your boyfriend, a CPPD detective, pull you away from an altercation with him?

"That doesn't mean I killed him!" I tell her.

Miranda steers me away from the growing crowd of reporters and looky-loos. The group has grown significantly since we located the body. What are these people doing here, anyway? Has the whole town heard about this already?

"Why don't we just walk over here for a bit?" she suggests.

"You're right. I get so frustrated with the way they insinuate things. How could they think I'd kill Herb to win the election?"

"You know how it goes. The more dramatic the story, the more people will tune in. Just shake it off," Miranda reminds me.

"Hey, did you check the body for magic traces? I didn't get a chance to." I ask her.

She nods her head. "I did. I couldn't find anything."

"Okay, so at least we know he was killed by a Non Supernatural."

"I would assume so," Miranda says. "Although good luck explaining that to anyone else."

Miranda, Damien, and I huddle together while we watch the police department work the crime scene. Tom took Poppy and Bubbles home. Fortunately, Poppy slept through the entire thing anyway and didn't realize what happened. Miranda and Damien continue to tell the reporters that I won't have anything further to say until I release an official statement tomorrow morning.

"What is my official statement?" I ask Damien.

"Beats me," he shrugs his shoulder. "It just seemed like something we should say."

"You'll tell everyone that you are deeply disturbed by what appears to be an act of violence against your opponent, but you have every faith in the Crested Peaks Police Department that they won't rest until they locate the killer bringing him or her to justice," Miranda tells us while we stare at her in awe.

"Maybe you should be the one running for office," I tell her.

"Not for a million dollars!" she laughs.

"What happens now that your opponent is dead?" Damien asks.

I shake my head. "Drew asked the same thing. I don't know. I suppose the Elections Division will let me know tomorrow."

"I wonder if *they* even know. You think anything like this has ever happened?" Miranda asks.

"Part of me hopes this hasn't happened before, and yet part of me doesn't want to be the only one that it has happened to," I tell them.

When Drew approaches us, the reporters fix their cameras on our group, eagerly anticipating something exciting.

"We'll be here all night," he explains, indicating the activity centering around Herb's body. "You should go home. Try to get some sleep."

When we realize it's already 2 AM, Damien and I groan. We'll get little sleep tonight regardless of everything that has happened this evening.

"Can you tell us anything?" I ask. "Who could have done this?"

Drew glances back at the crime scene and then at the reporters. Everyone stares at him to see what might happen. "Not here." He shakes his head. "Not right now. Make sure she gets home, you two. Keep her away from the reporters."

Damien and Miranda nod, steering me away from the crowd and back to the cafe. How could this happen two years in a row? A murder on Halloween. This time in a graveyard. Can't we just be normal around here? Why can't we be like everyone else? I'm certain other small mountain towns don't have these types of problems.

Chapter 3

The following morning, I arrive at work extra tired. Waking up at o'dark thirty - breakfast cafe time - is never easy. But when I barely sleep the night before, it's even worse.

I suggested we close the cafe today, but Damien convinced me it would be better to open. We want everyone to think it's business as usual. He's worried that some would find it suspicious if we closed. He doesn't want anyone to claim that I'm hiding at home.

Thankfully, he has plenty of coffee waiting for me when I arrive. Like always, Gladys, one of Marcall's long-time customers, arrives at 6:30, eager for her vegan breakfast burrito and coffee.

She's a tall, thin woman with fuzzy gray hair who has been a regular at Marcall's from the beginning. We don't even wait for her to order; Damien has it waiting for her every day.

She's always dressed impeccably, which is impressive for 6:30 AM! I'd swear she was a high-powered executive in a luxurious office, or perhaps even a fashion model.

She's never without gloves and a hat, which often match. She doesn't know it, but seeing her clothes closet someday is on my bucket list. It must be enormous. Maybe she has several. Or, even better, an entire room devoted just to her outfits and accessories.

"Good morning, everyone. I take it you didn't get much sleep last night," she says as Damien places her breakfast order in front of her. She snaps her stylish black gloves inside her matching silk purse.

"A couple of hours, if that," I explain, shaking my head.

"I can't believe this happened two years in a row," Damien laments.

"In case you were wondering, Herbert Appleton has four ex-wives--" Gladys begins.

"Gladys, let me stop you right now. You know I can't get into this. The guy was my political opponent!" I insist.

"I understand that my dear, it's just that I know how you often rely on my, er, special knowledge to help you solve these things, so I'm offering before you even ask this time."

Gladys is known as the town gossip. I don't mean that in the negative sense either. Not really, anyway. She just knows everything that goes on here. She's also been a tremendous help with solving the previous mysteries in town.

"You know I'm grateful for your past help--"

"I know things the CPPD doesn't know," she reminds me.

"I realize that, but I won't need your help with this. I won't need anyone's help because I won't get involved."

"Whatever you say, dear," she says, taking a sip of her coffee.

Why doesn't anyone believe me when I say these things?

"She still lives nearby." She continues as if I didn't just tell her I'm not getting involved. "She stars in that reality show Mountain Ex Wives."

"The one they film in Vail?" I ask.

"The very same." She nods her head.

I'm so fascinated by this idea that I momentarily forget I've refused to investigate. Reality TV is Marshall, Marcus, Stumpy, and my guilty pleasure. The rabbits maintain a hilarious and, of course, sarcastic dialogue throughout each episode. I admit it; we get invested in these peoples' lives.

Imagine my shock last year when Gladys discovered two reality show contestants hiding in the mountains of Crested Peaks. A couple that wasn't even supposed to be together because the star had proposed to a different contestant on tv!

We knew what happened before the final episode aired, thanks to Gladys' penchant for *all* news. I was so shocked when they stopped in the cafe one day for breakfast, I couldn't think of anything to say. It came out sounding like bleep bloop blop. It was my embarrassing Ralphie meets Santa Claus moment.

Now I find out that the fourth ex-wife of my deceased political opponent is a reality show star. Also, a suspect according to Gladys.

"Why do you think she could have killed him?" I ask, even when the voice in my head warns me not to.

"They went through a highly contentious divorce," she explains. "Lots of well-publicized arguments, plus she trashes him on the show constantly!"

"Oh my gosh," Damien exclaims. "I just remembered an episode!" He searches eagerly on his phone. "Here it is. It's on the internet." He shows us a video clip of Herb's ex-wife where the ladies on the show went axe-throwing for the day.

Tilly is waving her axe around and shouting about how it was too bad Herb wasn't nearby because if she had the chance, she'd throw it at him. We gawk at each other, wide-eyed.

"Told you!" Gladys responds smugly.

"Do you think she killed Herb?" I ask. "Wait! No!" I wave my hands in the air. "Don't answer that. If either of you has already forgotten, I'm not investigating this murder! The police will discover this on their own. Better yet, you can show them the video, Damien!"

Damien and Gladys nod at each other like now they really don't believe me.

"I don't care if you don't believe me! I'm not doing it. I won't get involved."

Chapter 4

The cafe is busy throughout the morning. It's a combination of customers who need a hearty breakfast burrito to appease their Halloween hangover plus curiosity seekers who heard about what happened last night and want to see for themselves if the dead guy's political opponent showed up for work. It was a good call on Damien's part - insisting that we open the cafe today. If not, tongues would wag far more than they already are.

I sent a press release to the media like Miranda advised last night in the graveyard. I pointed out that we were shocked and horrified by the senseless act of violence but have every confidence that the CPPD will solve the case as soon as possible.

In the middle of the morning, a round man with a graying comb-over and grumpy expression approaches me in the cafe. I recognize him as one of the county commissioners.

"Ms. Duffin, may I have a word, please?"

"Of course," I respond as we step to the side to talk privately. As privately as one can talk in a busy breakfast cafe, anyway.

"After last night, I'm sure you're wondering what happens next."

"Yes, I am. Obviously, I'm dismayed by what happened, but we're only a week away from the election, and I don't know where we go from here."

"Yes, I read your press release." He pinches his lips together. What a dour man. "I'm sure you can imagine we've never dealt with this kind of thing before."

I nod my head. "I was wondering about that."

"We dusted off some very old rules to search for the answer. We weren't even sure we had a contingency for this type of thing."

"And?" I ask eagerly. Obviously, I'm not excited about what happened, but I'm anxious to learn about the race's fate. Do we have to start over and hold the election some other time? I'm not eager to continue with the drama.

"The election continues as planned," the commissioner explains.

"But how?" I ask in surprise. Will someone pretend to be my opponent? How would that work? Could they even find someone that quickly? "Do we still vote next week?"

"We sure do," he nods his head vigorously.

"But who will I run against?"

"The ballots were already approved and printed, with yours and Appleton's name on them so you're still running against him."

"This is confusing," I admit. "What happens if Herb wins?" I make air quotes around the word wins.

"If your opponent wins, the county commissioners will choose someone to fill in until the next election."

"What if I win?" I ask.

"You win fair and square. You'll be Crested Peaks' newest mayor," he explains.

I didn't expect him to say that. It's hardly fair. It's not my fault that Herb is dead, but it's also strange that I'm running against a dead guy.

Do I campaign as usual until election day? I didn't even consider these things last night when I was pondering what happens next.

What if I win? Will people accuse me of cheating? What if Herb wins? Then I face the fact I couldn't beat a dead guy? Why is politics so complicated?

"I've heard of dead people voting but never one winning an election," I joke.

The commissioner stares back at me unblinkingly. Tough crowd.

"In that case, one could say she had a motive to kill her opponent, couldn't they?" a strange uptight-looking woman in a gray suit with pink pinstripes asks. Did she just listen to our entire conversation?

"Um, can I help you?" I ask her crossly. Who does she think she is listening to us then saying I had a motive to kill Herb?

"Charlotte Duffin?" she asks, flashing a CPPD badge. "Detective Thomas from the CPPD."

"What can I do for you?" I ask again.

"I'd like to ask you some questions about last night."

"Errr, okay," I stammer. I'm so confused. Who is this so-called detective? Where is Drew?

I swivel to the county commissioner to excuse myself, but I notice he's already slinking out the door. Figures.

"I'm investigating Herb Appleton's murder. Can you explain how your fingerprints ended up on the hatchet buried in your opponent's back?"

"*My* fingerprints? You're joking. That's impossible."

"Are you saying the hatchet we found in Mr. Appleton doesn't belong to you?" she presses.

"That's exactly what I'm saying! I assure you; my hatchet is at home in my garage where it's supposed to be."

"When was the last time you *think* you saw it?" she asks.

"There's no *think* about it; I used it last week to cut off some branches from the apple tree for my rabbits."

"Did someone say apple sticks?" Marshall asks, appearing out of thin air from the back room.

I ignore him. I'm certain this detective, whoever she is, won't find a conversation with the rabbits amusing.

"Then you're admitting to owning a hatchet like we found in Mr. Appleton?"

"Yes," I hesitate. "I guess. I think so." Oh dear, this is going sideways fast. I remember thinking the hatchet from last night looked like mine, but I can't be entirely sure. It was dark, after all.

"Where's Detective Bailey?" Damien asks, joining me at my side. I'm grateful for the support. This detective, who I've never seen, makes me nervous. Obviously, my hatchet is at home in the same place I last left it, but I don't like what this woman is insinuating.

"Detective Bailey is on desk duty until further notice."

"What? Why?" I shriek. If I thought I was uncomfortable before, now I'm on the verge of breathing into a paper bag.

"The department is aware of your relationship with Detective Bailey, in addition to your uncanny knack for finding dead bodies. There's also the matter of your frequent interference in CPPD cases."

"How dare you insult Detective Bailey!" Damien shouts.

"This is beyond awful," I whisper to him. "His job means everything to Drew."

"I tell you what," I say to the detective. "I'll take you to my house right now and show you that my hatchet is in the garage where I left it."

Detective Thomas nods her head and smiles. "I'll drive."

"Woo hoo!" Marcus shouts. "We're riding in a cop car!"

"No!" I point at him. "You're staying here!"

Detective Thomas is alarmed that I'm scolding a rabbit. A rabbit who's also freely running around the restaurant. I could explain to her that I use a spell that keeps the restaurant free from rabbit and cat hair. But it's none of her business.

"Make sure they stay here," I tell Damien, pointing at Marcus.

"Boss, are you sure you want to do this?" he asks.

"Yes!" I insist. "I'll show her," I jab my thumb in her direction, "that my hatchet is at home. I don't know how my fingerprints are on the one that killed Herb. I'm sure it's a big misunderstanding that we'll clear up as soon as possible."

I tell Detective Thomas how to get to my house but then we ride in silence the remainder of the trip. I know she thinks that if she remains quiet, I'll feel the urge to fill in the ride with talk and might slip up and say something incriminating. But there's nothing to slip up with.

I'm furious they're doing this to Drew and desperate to talk to him, but I don't want Detective Thomas to know that. It isn't lost on me that just a couple of years ago, when it looked like I killed the landlord for Marcall's building, I rode in a car just like this one to the CPPD station with Drew. I feel sick that he's on desk duty because of me. Sometimes I wonder why he even stays with me, given the trouble I cause him.

When we pull up in front of my house Detective Thomas stares at me like she's convinced she has called my bluff. But there's no bluff to call. I can't wait to wipe that smug look off her face when I show her the hatchet is exactly where I said it was.

When Gran died, I got her all-brick Queen Anne house complete with a massive wraparound porch, perfect for Sunday morning coffee, periwinkle blue window shutters and trim, and one of my favorite parts, a round turret that overlooks the town from the second story.

I punch in the code for the garage door while it opens slowly, sunlight flooding the space. For good measure I flick the light switch to add illumination so the detective can't miss the hatchet hanging on the wall. I cross my arms over my chest looking down at her with the most confident look I can manage. Won't she be disappointed when she sees...

Chapter 5

It's not here!

So much for wiping the smug look from the Detective's face.

"Oh, no!" I cry. "Just a moment! It's here somewhere. It has to be."

I frantically rifle through boxes and scan the walls. The hatchet always hangs on the wall above my workbench.

"Missing something?" she sneers.

"No!" I snap. "I've obviously misplaced it." But I distinctly remember hanging it back where I always do.

I purposely store it where the rabbits can't reach because I left it out once, and they gnawed on the handle. It isn't enough that I cut branches off the apple trees in the yard for them to chew on. They'll chew on any random thing when the mood strikes - if it's within reach.

Detective Thomas stares at me for several minutes while I continue my frantic search. She clears her throat. "Your hatchet isn't here because you used it to kill Herb Appleton last night in the graveyard."

"I did not!" I have the urge to stomp my foot; I'm so frustrated. "Am I under arrest?" I gulp.

Why can't Drew be here? This is far worse than when the CPPD thought I killed my landlord. Far worse than any of the other bodies they've found me with.

The detective sighs. She's disappointed. Did she expect me to confess on the spot? "I'm not arresting you *at this time* because the only evidence I have so far are your fingerprints on the murder weapon. Numerous witnesses tell me they saw you standing on the debate podium when Mr. Appleton was killed. But I assure you I'll figure out how you did it. Also, just so you know, I am aware of your," she pauses for effect, "talents," she adds, sneering at me.

She better not be talking about the fact I'm a witch. I've found most people in Crested Peaks to be very accepting of the paranormal. But like my recently deceased opponent and now maybe the detective, some continue to cling to the old ways.

Witches and ghosts and a variety of Supernaturals have always existed here, but in the past, they weren't accepted like they are now. Gran hid her gift for a long time. But not for the same reasons I did.

"Will you need a ride back to the cafe?" she asks.

"No, I won't need a ride back to the cafe. Thank you very much." Dangit. Of course, I need a ride back to the cafe. But I'm not telling her that.

"Suit yourself," she says, marching out to her car, her designer high heels clicking against the pavement. "Oh, and Ms. Duffin," she twists back, pausing. "I run my cases far different from your boyfriend, so don't even think about interfering in this."

"Fat chance of that," I mutter.

"What's that?" she asks.

"You have a lovely day, detective," I say, giving her my most practiced campaign smile.

She narrows her eyes at me, spins around, and continues her march to her car.

Chapter 6

I refuse to let her see me any more frantic than she already has, so I stand like a statue in the middle of my garage while I watch her car turn the corner. Then I tear apart the garage like a woman possessed.

After 20 minutes of searching, everything is in shambles, but no hatchet. I've upended the drawers, cleared the shelves, and emptied the boxes—all to no avail.

Where is that stupid thing? Is it possible that someone actually used it to kill Herb? But who? How would they get it out of my garage? Why would they try to set me up like this?

This is a nightmare. I didn't want to contact Drew in front of the detective, but now that she's gone, I'll take my chances.

Me: What's going on? Are you okay?

Drew: Yeah, I'm okay. Can't talk now, and you shouldn't say any more. I'll bring dinner over tonight when I get off work. Italian?

Me: Yes!

I desperately want to call him, but I suspect they're watching him like a hawk at the police station, and I don't want to get him in any more trouble than I already have.

My next text is to Miranda.

Me: Can I get a ride back to Marcall's?

Miranda: OMG, Damien told me everything. Are you at the police station? Did they arrest you?

Me: No, I'm still at my house.

Miranda: I'll be right there!

I could walk back to work. It's not that far, after all. But I need a friend right now.

When Miranda pulls up to the house in her Volvo station wagon, she barely has time to put it in park before she leaps from it and runs up the driveway.

"Charlotte! What happened? Did the cops do this? Shouldn't they clean up?"

If it's possible, I think Miranda is even more upset than me. I explain everything that happened since I saw her last night.

"Do you think someone set you up for Herb's murder?" she asks.

"That's the million-dollar question. But I'm not just leaving this up to the police - I don't care what Detective Thomas says."

"You're darn right! We've solved cases before; we'll solve this too!" she exclaims, pounding her fist into her hand.

"Let's go back to the cafe to discuss this with Damien. I also want to see if the rabbits are hiding the hatchet."

"Why would the rabbits hide your hatchet?" she asks.

"You know how they love to play tricks on me, so I hope that's the case this time. Except they'd need help to reach it. I usually hang it over that workbench because none of them can jump that high," I explain, pointing to a spot above the bench. "The rabbits are too small, and Stumpy only has two feet."

"Fine, but we're cleaning up your garage first," Miranda insists.

"That will take too long," I complain.

"Not when you're a witch."

"How do I keep forgetting that?" I smack myself on the forehead.

"I don't know, but c'mon help me put everything back."

Miranda and I then use our magical powers, returning everything to its rightful place within minutes. After that, we drive back to Marcall's, where Damien rushes us as we walk in the door.

"Boss!" he shouts. "What happened? I was sure you'd be right back after you showed your hatchet to that wretched detective!"

"It wasn't there."

His face pales. "Then where is it?"

"I don't know." I throw my hands up.

"This is awful," he moans in distress. "What are we going to do now?"

"Are the boys here?"

"They were in the back napping last time I checked," he responds, looking confused about why I've suddenly switched to asking about the animals.

"Marshall! Marcus! Stumpy!" I bellow. No time for niceties right now. They scramble from the back room.

"Did you bring parsley?" Marshall asks.

"No. Listen, I need you to--"

"Why not?" Marcus chimes in.

"Why not, what?"

"Why didn't you bring parsley?" Marshall continues to ask.

"Because I'm too busy to worry about your parsley at the moment," I snap at them. "You'll get some for dinner."

The rabbits roll their eyes at each other, then head back to their nap area to continue what I so rudely interrupted.

"Wait! I didn't finish!" I insist.

Stumpy stares at Marshall and Marcus, then me. He isn't sure he wants to get involved in this.

"You know the hatchet I use to cut apple branches for you?"

"The one you keep up high so we can't reach it?"

"Yes! That's the one!" I exclaim excitedly. I hope they're about to tell me they know where it is. Or that they got it down and have hidden it. "Do you know where it is?"

They eye each other with puzzled expressions. "It's above the workbench where you always put it," Marshall says.

"No, it isn't," I tell them.

"What did you do with it?" Marcus asks accusingly.

"I did nothing!" I'm practically shouting at them now. "I need to know if you did!"

"But you hang it out of our reach on purpose," Marshall reminds me.

"I get -- never mind." They obviously don't know where it is or why I'm questioning them. "I was just wondering."

"She's so weird," Marshall says to Marcus while they nod their heads and wander back to my office to resume their naps.

"They don't know where it is," I explain to the others.

"I hate to say this, boss, but I think someone used your hatchet to kill Herb," Damien says.

"How is that even possible?" I lament. "That means someone got into my garage without my knowing, stole it, then killed Herb on purpose to frame me!"

"So, we start with the usual," he offers.

"Which is?"

"Gladys told you about ex-wife number four," he reminds me.

"Oh, that's right. I can't believe it was just this morning. When I refused to get involved." I sigh. "No matter how much I swear I'm not doing this, somehow I always get sucked in."

"Ain't that the truth." Damien shakes his head.

"Ex-wife number four? Who is that?" Miranda asks.

"You know who she is, Tilly Rock on the Bored Rich Housewives tv show," Damien tells her.

"Oh, my gosh!" Miranda exclaims. "A producer was in the coffee shop this morning saying they're filming in Crested Peaks today, but I didn't make the connection then."

"Seriously? Why are they here today?" I can't believe this fell into our laps so easily.

"I bet because of Herb's death. The show knows it would provide plenty of drama," Miranda points out.

"But where are they filming?" I ask.

"That I don't know."

"I bet Harvey knows," Damien says.

"Next to Gladys, he knows everything," Aranya reminds us as she walks in the front door.

"I'm really glad to see you!" I tell her.

"I'm sorry I couldn't get here sooner. I had a test this morning."

"That's okay. I'm happy you're here now. You two can mind the cafe while Miranda and I see Harvey," I tell them.

I catch Damien shaking his head out of the corner of my eye. He gets so nervous when we do things like this.

"You're the one who reminded me about the fourth ex-wife and Harvey!" I point at him accusingly.

"Don't remind me," he sighs.

Chapter 7

Miranda and I quickly return to her car and drive to the Hotel Glacier.

The entire town of Crested Peaks is one long street with a single traffic light. Quaint shops line both sides of Main Street. They're so cute you'd swear you were in a Hallmark Christmas movie special. Except our snow is real!

Harvey has been so helpful in the past when we need assistance solving a mystery. As a ghost, he sees and hears things that ordinary people don't, and living at the hotel gives him a unique vantage point.

He was the manager when they built the hotel in the late 1800s but got caught in a shootout between the sheriff and a bank robber. He tells us he was so busy at the hotel that, rather than going into the light, he just stayed on to continue working.

I feel bad because I haven't visited him lately. He often claims we only show up when we need answers, so each time I vow I'll come back soon just to say hello. But then the cafe gets busy, and I forget. Hopefully, he isn't cross with us today.

Miranda and I run toward the hotel entrance with our fingers crossed, hoping it will be easy to find him. We're lucky because Harvey is out front directing guests to the check-in desk.

He wears the outfit he was killed in, of course. The 19th-century hotel manager's uniform consisting of a dark gray suit coat with tails and a vest. He likes to point out that he should be wearing a top hat, but it fell off when he got shot. He says if he'd known he was going to die, he would have insisted that someone put it back on his head before he expired.

Tourists come from all around hoping to glimpse a ghost at the hotel. Then they're surprised and delighted to discover it's far more than a glimpse and that they might even have a conversation with one.

"My dear ladies!" Harvey exclaims when he sees us. "What brings you here on this crisp autumn afternoon?"

"We have questions, Harvey."

"Ahhh, let me guess. It's about the untimely demise of your political nemesis." He *tsks*. "Politics is an ugly business."

"I'm beginning to see that!" I nod my head.

"Sadly, it's always been that way. Even way back in my day."

"That's depressing," Miranda responds.

"I agree," he says. "Now, how can I be of assistance, my fair maidens?"

"We understand they're in town filming Bored Rich Housewives today."

"Ah yes, the production crew was in the lobby bright and early. They hoped to check in early but were most disagreeable when they discovered that couldn't happen until later in the day."

"Do you know where they're filming?" I ask.

"I believe they were starting in the graveyard where they found Herb's body. I heard them say they thought that was where the most dramatic footage would be," he tells us.

"Great! We have to go!" I exclaim.

"Wait! That's it? You only want to know about the film crew? You never come just to say hello," Harvey whines.

"I know. I swear we'll be back one of these days just to chat, okay?"

"But you always say that!" he reminds me.

"We really mean it this time!" Miranda exclaims while we race back to her car with Harvey glowering at us.

"We should have guessed it would be the cemetery, right?" Miranda points out.

We arrive at the graveyard, and just as Harvey said, several trucks are in the parking lot. It must be the production crew. We leave the car and walk toward where they found Herb's body.

I shiver at the thought of seeing that again. It freaks me out to think that it might truly be my hatchet that killed him. I'm fortunate that all those people saw me in the cafe, walking to the graveyard, then standing on the podium, or I could be in a lot more trouble than I already am.

Miranda and I wait on the sidelines, watching the crew film Tilly surveying the yellow crime scene tape surrounding the area where we found her ex-husband's body. My stomach ties in knots, seeing it in the daylight. There's a dark spot on the ground where we found him.

Tilly looks so forlorn, staring at the area. She wipes away a tear, and I feel for her. Maybe after all this time, she still loves him. Despite the public arguments. Who knows what goes on in private?

Then the director yells, "Cut! Let's take five, everybody!"

"Where are my cigarettes?" Tilly shouts. "I need a cigarette! Yo! Boy!" she screams at a petrified-looking young man. "Get me a cigarette right now!" she snaps her fingers while he hurries away, looking relieved he has an excuse to leave.

"What are you staring at?" she then shouts at a cameraman.

Miranda and I gawk at each other. Talk about a 180. A moment ago, she had what appeared to be a personal emotional moment, and the second they shut off the cameras, she's barking orders at anyone within reach.

"I did *not* expect that," Miranda mutters.

"It's now, or never, I guess," I whisper as we approach Tilly. Now I'm scared of what she'll do.

"Excuse me, Tilly?" I ask.

"Whaddya want?" she growls.

"I'm Char--"

"Oh! Wait! I know who you are! My apologies. I thought you were just some dumb gopher who can't seem to find me a dadgum cigarette!" she screams over her shoulder. "You're running against my ex-husband for mayor. Or you were anyway." She laughs. "Guess you solved that problem, didn't you?"

"I'm so sorry for your loss," I tell her.

She snorts. "Some loss. Hey," she leans in close, "is it true you did it? Did you kill the scumbag? What did it feel like? More importantly, why didn't you invite me?" she cackles.

"Of course, I didn't kill him!" I respond indignantly.

"Seriously? They said you led the cops right to his body. How else would you know exactly where to go?" she says, pointing at the area behind her.

"It's a long story," I tell her.

"Look, sister, I don't blame you. Herb was a lousy human being. You wouldn't be the first person who wanted to stick something sharp in him. You would just be the first person to actually do it!" She scream-laughs with such intensity I cringe. "And the last!" she shrieks even louder with laughter, then claps my back so hard I nearly stumble.

Tilly is a tall woman. Taller than me, it appears. Even without the spiky high heels. She's what Gran would have called big-boned. She also has the biggest hair I've ever seen.

They piled her dyed blonde hair high on her head, making me wonder how much hairspray her stylist must go through in a day. Her filled lips are painted a deep ruby red to match her claw like fingernails. Fingernails I certainly wouldn't want to get into a fight with.

"I swear to you I didn't do it! But I need to find out who did!" I protest.

"Okay, okay, I believe you. So, what can I do for you?" she asks.

"Where were *you* when Herb was killed?" I ask.

"Ohhh, I get it!" She shakes with laughter once again. She enjoys this for a person who just lost someone they were once married to. "You think *I* killed Herb."

"I'm just looking into every possibility."

"As much as I *wanted* to kill him, I was at a Halloween charity event in Vail. The camera crew recorded everything. "Didn't you guys?" she shouts at them while they look half-scared to answer. "I'll get footage of the event for you if you want."

"That would be great, thank you." We nod our heads. If it's true that she had a camera crew following her all evening, that rules her out right away. Rats. Why is this always so hard? Why can't someone just confess immediately?

"If you're looking for legitimate suspects, ladies, I'd try Ted Carter."

"Oh? Who is that?" I ask.

"He was a tenant in one of Herb's dumpy rentals. He insists that there was mold in the property that Herb refused to clean up, making him sick. He sued but lost big time. It's even rumored that the judge was one of Herb's pals.

"The guy lost his job, and his wife left him because she was so tired of it all. Top that off with the lawsuit bankrupting him. As much as *I* wanted to stick Herb with something sharp, I'd say Ted wanted it even more."

"Good to know; thanks for the tip!" I tell her.

But just as Miranda and I prepare to leave, I hear a familiar voice. "Ms. Duffin."

Shoot. I was hoping we wouldn't run into her. "Detective Thomas." I nod at her.

"What are you doing here?" she asks.

"Just watching them film Bored Rich Housewives. That's perfectly legal," Miranda snaps at her.

"It is if that's all you're doing. But considering we're at the crime scene, along with the woman who just happens to be the victim's ex-wife, I find your explanation hard to swallow."

"So. We're fans of the show," Miranda tells her.

"*I* think you're interfering with my investigation, despite my telling you not to."

"Not at all, detective. We were just leaving," I assure her.

"I meant what I said, Charlotte! You're not to interfere in this!" she shouts after us.

I nod my head and wave back at her as we walk away. Getting lectured by someone other than Drew about interfering with an investigation is a little weird. Now I'm more worried than ever about what they're doing to him back at the station.

If this jeopardizes his career, I'll never forgive myself. He's worked hard to become a detective in such a short time, and I know my interference in his work often gets him in trouble with his superiors. We have to be careful about how we investigate from now on.

Chapter 8

When Miranda and I return to the café, Damien and Aranya eagerly await our news.

"What did she say?" Damien asks, "Please tell me she confessed!"

"You know, it's never that easy," I remind him.

"I know, but somehow I always hope."

"What was it like? Did you see them filming?" Aranya asks.

"It was interesting," Miranda replies.

"Uh, oh. What does that mean?" Aranya says, confusion crossing her face.

"Reality TV is definitely staged," Miranda tells her.

"Oh my gosh, spill!"

"Let's just say Tilly is one person while the cameras are rolling – –" I start.

"--and another when they're off!" Miranda finishes with a shudder.

"But did she have an alibi?" Damien asks.

"She says she was at a charity event in Vail," I tell him.

"With cameras following her every move," Miranda adds.

"Well, dang," Damien snaps his fingers.

"She told us about one of Herb's former tenants, though, so I'll check him out as soon as possible," I explain.

We pause our discussion for the moment when a stranger walks in the door.

"Welcome to Marcall's!" Aranya greets him.

"Why, if it isn't Charlotte Duffin!" he exclaims.

"Yes?" I respond in confusion. I don't recognize him. Maybe he's one of my supporters? A campaign volunteer? It's been such a busy time, and I've talked to so many people it's easy to get them mixed up. "I'm sorry. Have we met? At a campaign event?"

"I don't blame you for not remembering! The last time I saw you, you were this high." He holds his hand a few feet from the ground.

What on earth is this guy talking about?

"I'm a friend of your parents!" he then exclaims.

"I see," I tell him. That is so not what I wanted to hear.

Damien's eyes practically bug out of his head while Aranya is worried. I'm concerned for a moment that Miranda might hex him; she stares at him so angrily.

"What can I do for you, Mr....?"

"Oops, sorry about that. My name is Charles Hardy, but you can call me Chuck."

"As I'm sure you know, Mr. Hardy, my parents passed away many years ago."

He nods. "I saw in the newspaper that your grandma passed a couple of years ago as well. I was very sorry to learn that. She was a good woman, your grandma."

"Yes, she was," I murmur.

"Did you sell her huge house?" he asks.

"No, I still live there."

"Seriously? That's a big home for one person!"

Who complains about the size of someone's house? How is that any of his business?

"Is there something we can help you with, Mr. Hardy?" Miranda asks, looking crosser by the moment.

"I just wanted to stop in to say hello. I'm in town on business, in case you were wondering."

"We weren't," Miranda growls. She sure is feisty. But her hostile attitude doesn't phase him one bit.

"Hey, I also saw that you're running for mayor! That's so cool. Your parents would be proud," he continues.

I give him a weak smile. Yeah, my parents would've seen this as a great way to fleece the unsuspecting citizens of Crested Peaks. Even more than they did back in the day, anyway.

"I don't mean to be rude, Mr. Hardy, but we're getting ready to close for the day, which means I have a lot of work to do otherwise, so _ _"

"Oh! Say no more! I'll get out of your hair; I just wanted to let you know that you're doing a great job here with this obviously successful café and your grandma's big house!"

"Yeah, yeah, thanks so much for stopping by," Miranda says, her voice heavy with sarcasm as she opens the door to usher him out.

"I'll stop in for breakfast before I leave town!" he tells us, stepping onto the sidewalk.

"You do that," Miranda says, flipping the sign to close while she shuts and locks the door. "The nerve of that guy!" she complains.

"There's only one kind of business he'd be in town for," I grumble.

"Do you think he really was a friend of your parents?" Aranya asks.

"He seems sleazy enough!" Damien adds.

"Obviously, I don't remember him, but the fact that he acts like being a friend of my parents is something to boast about tells me he was one of their criminal friends."

"Why did he keep pressing you about the house?" Miranda asks. "He must think you have a ton of money."

"Hopefully, he leaves town before I have to see him again."

"Maybe he'll get arrested," Damien offers.

"That's always a good possibility with that crowd!" I tell him. "Anyway, where were we?" I pretend I have more important things to think about than my parents' former acquaintance, but I'm more rattled about this than I want to admit, even to myself.

I wish I could believe this is a coincidence, but I'm running for office, *and* I'm the prime suspect in a murder, *then* a stranger shows up prattling on about my house and the cafe. This can't be good.

"Back to Tilly. Do we have proof that she was at the charity event like she claims?" Aranya asks.

Miranda nods her head. "She told us she'd get the footage to prove it."

"That's too bad. I mean that she has a solid alibi, otherwise I'd consider her to be the primary suspect. She complained about their nasty divorce on a bunch of episodes of Bored Rich Housewives," Aranya adds.

"What if she *paid* someone to kill Herb?" Damien practically whispers it as if someone else might overhear. "Like your parents' friend!" he exclaims wide-eyed.

"Oh, that's all I need!" I moan.

We discuss our next steps for a while longer, including making plans to track down Herb's tenant tomorrow, but when Marshall, Marcus, and Stumpy get impatient, we call it a day. I help the boys into my old Prius, and we drive home.

The idea that someone may have been in my garage, and possibly even my house, makes me nervous. Who could have done that without my knowing? I vow to check *everything* to make sure nothing else is missing.

As if I didn't have enough to worry about, now I have to wonder why Charles Hardy is in town and could it really relate to Herb's murder? Why does everything always go haywire? Can't we just be normal for once?

Chapter 9

I await anxiously for Drew to arrive with dinner. I'm so nervous. It will be good to see him because it's unusual to go an entire day without talking to him or having him pop into the café for donuts when he's nearby. But I'm worried about what he'll have to say about work.

"I am so sorry!" I cry out when I open the door.

"I know, it's okay. It's not your fault," he reassures me.

"But I'm the one who keeps getting mixed up in these situations, and now I've dragged you into it!"

Upon realizing Drew is here, Marshall, Marcus, and Stumpy run to him for the customary treats he always brings.

"You guys!" I scold them. "Drew has far better things to do right now than worry about treats for you."

But of course, he remembers catnip for Stumpy and pansies for the rabbits. Stumpy immediately flops on his side, rolling in the catnip, and purring like crazy. Marshall and Marcus chew noisily on their pansies while watching Stumpy.

"He is so weird!" Marshall says while Marcus nods his head.

"Does he realize how ridiculous he looks?" Marcus asks.

"The rabbits say thank you," I tell Drew while they roll their eyes at me.

I remove our dinner from the bags while Drew sets the table. We have a lot to discuss, but I'm famished. I wasn't sure I'd be able to eat because my stomach has been in knots all day.

But the moment I smell the eggplant parmesan and garlic bread, my stomach momentarily forgets our troubles, remembering lunch was an awfully long time ago.

"Give it to me straight," I tell Drew, pouring each of us a generous glass of Shiraz. "How much trouble are you in at work?"

He sighs, tying my stomach in knots again. "They're just going overboard on this case because of how it appears. They've pointed out that my girlfriend, who also happens to be running for public office, is involved in another murder. My lieutenant and the higher-ups want to ensure everything is on the up and up. They don't want even a hint of scandal or favoritism."

"So you aren't about to be fired?"

"Not if I do what they say."

"I'm just so sorry they've benched you. I know how important your job is to you. You've worked so hard to get where you are, and if you get fired or demoted, I'll never forgive myself. If it helps, I could withdraw from the race. They could start the entire process over."

"Don't be silly. It's not that bad." He hugs me. " Not yet, anyway. I'm sure Detective Thomas will find the killer, and this will all blow over."

"I assume you know I brought her here today to show her the hatchet that's mysteriously gone missing."

He nods gravely. "I'm not supposed to know, but yes, I'm aware of that. I have friends who have been filling me in on the side. Plus, you wouldn't believe how much I overhear when I'm just working quietly at my desk." He smiles. "I realize now how the rabbits always overhear things."

"The hatchet they found in Herb's back isn't mine, right? It can't be." I'm losing hope on that front, though. When Drew takes a deep breath, I know the news isn't good.

"I overheard another detective saying the handle has small teeth marks that they're trying to identify. I assume those belong to the rabbits, which, along with your fingerprints, means it must be your hatchet."

"I kept hoping it was just a big mistake," I whine.

"It's not. So not only do we have to find out who killed Herb, we need to find out why they want to frame you."

"We?" I ask in shock.

"We, the CPPD," he says.

"Oh. For a second, there--"

"Nice try. I also heard that Detective Thomas caught you talking to Tilly while the reality show was filming at the crime scene."

"Would you believe me if I told you we were just there watching?"

"No."

"Fine. I heard Tilly was Herb's fourth ex-wife and a potential suspect," I admit.

"Let me guess. Gladys."

"I never reveal my sources."

Drew rolls his eyes. He knows me too well. "What did Tilly say?"

"She was at a charity event in Vail when Herbert was murdered."

"Do they have video?" Drew asks.

"Yep!"

"That gives her a solid alibi, then."

"Unfortunately. For my sake, anyway. Oh, and to make this day even better, an old friend of my parents showed up at the café this afternoon."

"Excuse me?" Drew is as angry as Miranda was.

"He kept mentioning how big this house is and that my café is so successful."

"I don't like the sounds of that at all."

"He gave me the creeps." I shudder just thinking about it again.

"What's his name? I'll check him out."

I give Drew his name, which he enters into his phone. "The timing is fishy to me. We may want to consider him a suspect."

"Damien thought the same thing." I nod my head.

As we continue our fantastic dinner, I explain what happens with the election process.

"So, you're running against a dead guy at this point?" Drew asks.

"That about sums it up." I cut him off just as he opens his mouth to say something. "I already joked about dead people voting, but the county commissioner wasn't amused."

"Bummer," he laughs.

"It's a good joke," I point out.

"I certainly thought so."

I almost mention Ted Carter, Herb's tenant, as a potential suspect, but stop when I realize he'll just tell me to leave it to the police. I hate keeping things from him, but it's probably better that he doesn't know. That way, he can truthfully claim ignorance if his lieutenant asks. This is how I rationalize it, anyway.

After Drew leaves, I search for the tenant online. I should go to bed because I know I'll be tired in the morning, but with the election less than a week away, I'm running out of time.

I find numerous articles detailing Ted's dispute with Herb. He insists that living in one of Herb's "cheap slums," as he calls it, made him sick. He maintains he told Herb about it multiple times, but he ignored his pleas.

Ted even paid for a test with his own money, which came back high for mold. But when he confronted him about it publicly, Herb accused him of cheating and insisted he would get another test done.

However, it never happened. The fight then spilled onto social media, with Ted threatening to kill him over it. So that's two people I know of who have made death threats against Herb, I murmur to myself. He said Herb cost him his health, his job, and his marriage, and he deserves payback. No wonder Tilly said he could be a suspect.

When I find myself nodding off in front of the computer, I realize if I don't go to bed now, I'll really be sleepy at work tomorrow. Scratch that. It's 1 AM, so tomorrow is already here. Oh well. I should at least try to get a couple of hours of sleep and start fresh later, when I can talk this over with Damien.

Chapter 10

When I see Damien at work, I tell him what I learned last night about Ted Carter, along with my plans to question him.

"Are you sure this is OK with Drew?" Damien asks.

"Well..." I hesitate.

"Boss, you know how nervous I get when you question these suspects on your own."

"Yes, I know that, but Drew isn't even allowed to get near this, so it would be unfair of me to burden him with this information."

"Isn't that convenient? You should at least let Detective Thomas know then," he scolds.

"But I don't want to talk to her at all if I can avoid it. Besides, I bet she'll just dismiss it."

"Don't say I didn't warn you!" he waggles his finger at me.

"I never say that," I tell him. "Now I need to figure out where to find him."

Damien sighs. "Not that I'm encouraging you, but I bet Gladys knows."

"Oh, good idea. It's 6:25, so she should be here any sec--"

"Happy All Souls Day, everyone!" Gladys announces, walking into the cafe right on cue.

I'm not sure that "happy" is the proper greeting for the day, but not surprisingly, she's dressed in all black, including a fascinator with a small veil pinned on her head and sleek black gloves.

"We were just talking about you, Gladys."

"That's why my ears are warm," she says, placing her fingertips against her ear.

"Coming right up, Gladys!" Damien calls out from the back.

"How did your talk with Tilly go yesterday?" she asks.

When I look surprised, she responds. "I know everything, dear. But you already knew that."

"She has an alibi for when Herb was killed."

"That's too bad. For you anyway."

"She told us to check out Ted Carter, one of Herb's tenants," I tell her.

"Oh yes, another good possibility," she exclaims, smacking her hand on her knee for emphasis.

"Do you know where I can find him?" I ask.

"I believe he still lives in the house he rented from Herb."

"I thought he said it made him sick and ruined his life. Why would he still live there?"

Gladys shrugs. "Herb refused to let him out of the lease."

"With Herb dead, he won't have to worry about the lease anymore." I point out.

"Good observation," she responds.

"That and revenge could be motive," I muse.

It's easy to figure out Ted's address, given all the publicity he generated for himself, so when Aranya comes in later that morning, I take off for his place, hoping to catch him at home. At the last second, I grab some of our special donuts. I think he'll be much more likely to talk to me with sweets in hand. That way I can claim I'm campaigning.

I pull up in front of a house that's in disarray. The unruly yard is full of overgrown weeds, there's a broken down truck parked in the front yard, and the screen door has seen better days.

No wonder Tilly said the tenant was mad at Herb. As I approach the front door, there's a man, who I assume is Ted, struggling to get out, his arms weighed down by moving boxes. I run up to the door to hold it open for him.

"Hello!" I exclaim.

"Oh my goodness," he says. "You startled me!"

"Sorry about that. I didn't want you to drop anything. I'm Charlotte Duffin, and I'd like your vote for Crested Peaks Mayor," I tell him, thrusting the donuts in his direction after he places the boxes on the ground. "You're Ted Carter, right?"

"I am Ted Carter and I know exactly who you are!" he exclaims. "I'm one of your biggest supporters!"

"You are? That's fabulous. Thank you so much!"

"I bet you're glad to be rid of that dirtbag, Appleton, huh?"

"Oh, uh, well," is the only thing I can think to say.

"I know I am!" he exclaims happily.

"I heard you had some problems with him," I tell him.

"*Problems* is an understatement! I lost my health, my job, and my wife because of that guy! But now that he's dead, I'm finally free of this dump!" He makes a rude gesture toward the house.

"Why didn't you just leave before if it's so bad?" I ask.

He snorts. "I couldn't. Herb refused to fix the problems. Then he refused to let me out of my lease. I was stuck. I can't afford two leases. I can barely afford this one! If I quit paying and he evicted me, it would go on my record, and I wouldn't be able to rent another place even if I could afford it."

"You have a point there." I nod my head. I'm almost afraid to ask him where he was when Herb was killed. I don't want to add insult to injury. But I didn't come here to be delicate. "Can I ask you where you were when Herb was killed?"

"Did you forget already? I was at the debate! You even shook my hand. Your friend gave me one of those cool buttons she made!"

"Oh, yes, of course. There were just so many people that night."

"No doubt! I wouldn't really expect you to remember me, anyway. It must be hard with everyone you've met while campaigning."

"It has been a lot!" I admit.

"I was waiting for the debate to start along with everyone else, but then you wandered off for a bit. The next thing I knew, I heard people screaming, so I followed the crowd. There you were with Herb's body. I nearly cheered out loud. Then I saw that hatchet sticking out of his back, and I thought, man, I'd love to shake the hand of the fella who did that! When you find him, let me know so I can thank him."

"I'll try to remember that." I tell him, slowly backing away, hoping I don't stumble on the broken walkway. "But I appreciate your support."

"Don't forget to vote on Tuesday!" he calls out as I head back to my car.

"I won't!" I tell him.

"Vote early, vote often, eh?" he laughs. "Hey, wait! One more thing!" he adds, while I pause. "A lot of people hated Appleton, but one guy who may have hated him more than me is Frank Goodman."

"That name sounds familiar," I tell him.

"It should! He was one of Herb's cronies!"

"But why would he hate Herb?" I ask.

"Rumor has it that Frank's wife and Herb were extra friendly once upon a time. If you know what I mean." He makes an exaggerated wink at me.

"Oh! Well, thanks for the tip!" I tell him while continuing to my car. Once inside, I wave and quickly drive away. He's quite the oddball.

As I drive back to the cafe, I ponder our bizarre conversation. Ted certainly had motive, but did he have the means? Does he know where I live? He says he was at the debate, but what if he killed Herb and then came to the debate to give himself an alibi?

But if he's one of my biggest fans, then why would he go out of his way to frame me for murder? Time is flying, but I don't seem to be getting anywhere. Now I have to figure out where I can find this Frank Goodman.

Chapter 11

"**W**here do I find Frank Goodman?" I ask the rabbits. I'm kind of joking, but let's face it, they often know things that surprise me.

"You mean that guy who does those infomercials?" Marcus asks.

"The what?" I respond.

"Stumpy watches him on TV," Marshall tells us.

"What does he do on TV?"

Marshall stares at Stumpy. I always wonder what they say to each other. Part of me probably doesn't want to know. "He makes loans," he says, like that explains it all.

"What kind of loans?" I ask.

"He helps people buy homes."

"He's a mortgage broker?"

"Beats me. I just know what Stumpy saw on TV." Marshall shrugs.

"Here it is, boss." Aranya holds her phone out to me.

Of course, she's already searching online for him. What did we do before the internet? Apparently, he makes loans to help people buy short-term rental properties, which are extremely popular in mountain towns.

"Whoa, check out these reviews," Aranya adds.

According to the internet, Frank makes risky loans to people who can barely afford them. Then when they can't pay, he seizes the property for himself.

I peer over her shoulder and groan at the picture of him lounging on the couch playing video games. "I make money doing nothing all day. You can too!" The caption reads.

"Ugh." I cringe. "What a standup guy."

"There's more," Aranya points out. "A recent article talks about how he is pushing City Council to relax any ordinances regarding short-term rentals."

We need to ensure that the right people are elected this November. People who support our values. We have every right to purchase and enjoy rental property as we see fit. That's why I am supporting Herb Appleton for Crested Peaks Mayor.

"Did he say that before or after he found out Herb took up with his wife?" I ponder aloud.

"That's a good question," she says.

"Maybe he doesn't care. Maybe money wins out over the wife?" Damien suggests.

"I suppose that's possible." I surmise. "Although if he only recently discovered what was happening, that could be motive."

"But why set you up to take the fall?" Aranya asks.

"Take out two enemies at once?" I suggest.

"Maybe he thought he could get rid of Herb for betraying him, and a bonus was to frame you and get rid of you too? Take his chances on starting over with a new candidate," Aranya says. "Check it out! He's hosting a seminar at the community center today. It just started!" she points at her phone excitedly.

"Let's go!" I exclaim. "You can handle the café, right?" I ask Damien.

"If I say no, will you stay?" he responds.

Aranya raises an eyebrow at me.

"I didn't think so. Go," Damien says.

We giggle as we hurry out the door before he can change his mind and race to the community center. We find Frank making a flashy presentation to a packed room. He insists that with "very little down and even mediocre credit," he can get you a loan on a ski condo.

I'm surprised to learn that he also takes a portion of the rent the investor gets. That's besides the monthly loan payments, with absurdly high interest rates.

"No wonder he needs friends on the City Council," Aranya whispers.

The audience leans forward, eager to keep learning.

"He really pushes this idea of passive income, doesn't he?" I whisper back.

Aranya scowls. "I know little about mountain rentals, but are those profit amounts accurate? It's a bit high, isn't it?"

But as I nod my head, I realize Frank has stopped talking.

"You ladies seem eager to learn more." He points at us. "Can I answer any questions?" he asks as the entire room pivots to stare at us.

"We'd like documentation supporting your claims that you can actually get that much rent on one of those properties," Aranya demands.

"Aranya!" I hiss. I agree with her doubts about Frank's figures, but that's not why we're here.

"Why, of course! That's a great question. My staff can make sure we get those documents to you."

When Aranya raises her hand again, I clutch her arm, whispering in her ear, "Is this another question about the loans?"

"Yes!" she whispers back.

"That's not why we're here!" I remind her.

"I get that, but he's scamming these people!"

"Obviously, I understand that, but for now, we have a murder to solve in case you've forgotten!"

"Fine!" she pulls her arm down while I notice the relief on Frank's face.

We tolerate the rest of his high-energy presentation. I'm dismayed when so many clamor to talk to him at the end.

I understand wanting to make money by investing in real estate in Crested Peaks. But given his loan terms, they'd be better off seeking a loan elsewhere.

Unfortunately, I suspect most people here don't qualify for those kinds of loans, and Frank takes advantage of that.

His assistants are undoubtedly used to handling excited crowds, as they herd his fans into separate groups, while answering their questions, and passing out additional materials and loan applications.

Aranya and I weave our way through the crowd to approach him. "Hi, Frank. I'm Charlotte Duffin--"

"I know who you are." He gives me a pinched look. It's still hard to get used to all these people recognizing me.

"We'd like to talk to you about Herb Appleton," Aranya says.

His expressio grows increasingly bitter. "I knew you weren't here to learn about loans. Why haven't they arrested you for Herb's murder?"

Wow. Word travels so fast in this town.

"Because I didn't kill him. Besides, the police and other witnesses saw me on the debate stage when Herb was killed, giving me a solid alibi."

"I'm sure there are workarounds," he smirks.

"Care to tell us where *you* were when Herb was killed?" I ask.

"Not that it's any of your business, but I was relaxing in one of my rentals in Aspen."

"Is there anyone who can corroborate that story?" I ask him.

He shakes his head. "I went alone for some peace and quiet. I hate Halloween. All those kids running around shouting, banging on the door. It's so annoying. They don't do that in Aspen. At least not in the neighborhood my place is in."

"You can't tell us if anyone saw you there? A neighbor maybe?"

"What business is it of yours anyway?" he growls.

"We were just wondering," Aranya says with her hands up.

"Well, wonder somewhere else. I have work to do." He pushes me aside then walks over to a group of people waving loan applications in the air.

"One at a time, my friends!" he announces cheerfully. "You're well on your way to getting rich while you sleep!"

"You thought reality tv was staged," Aranya mutters.

"What kind of person hates Halloween?" I add.

Aranya and I drive back to the café in silence. The murder mystery and election weigh heavily on me. Frank claims he was in Aspen, and at this point, I can't prove he wasn't.

The same lingering question applies to him. Does he know where I live, and could he break into my garage to steal the hatchet? How would any of them know where to find it? None of this makes sense.

Obviously, I didn't kill Herb, but someone purposely stole my hatchet to frame me. Everyone I've talked to has a motive for murder, but what's their rationale for framing me?

When we arrive back at the café, I see Charles Hardy leaving Bean Around A Bit with a cup of coffee in his hand. He has his head down and walks quickly up Main Street. I stare at him, hoping he'll notice that I'm watching, but he doesn't look up.

"Hey, isn't that your parents' friend?" Aranya asks.

"Sure is," I respond. "Is it just me, or does he look suspicious?"

"I think no matter what he does, he'll look suspicious," she says.

"Fair enough. But I think he's looking extra suspicious at the moment," I explain.

"Hey, was that Charles Hardy I saw coming out of Miranda's place just now?" Damien asks the moment we walk in the door.

"It sure was," Aranya growls.

"He didn't come in here, did he?" I ask.

"Nope!" Damien shakes his head. What did you find out from Frank? "He confessed, right?"

I put my hands on my hips, sighing in his direction.

"I know, I know. It's never that easy."

We fill Damien in on what we just experienced with Frank.

"Well, this is so depressing," he grumbles. "What do we do next?"

"I'm not sure. Double-check everyone's alibis, I suppose. See if we can catch one of them in a lie," I tell them.

After we close the café for the day, I send Aranya home while I finish some long-neglected paperwork. I've been so busy with the campaign that I'm behind on a lot of chores for the café. Damien sticks around to work on a new recipe.

But after 20 minutes of distracted sighing, I give up. "I'm getting nowhere with this," I tell Marshall, Marcus, and Stumpy, who are sound asleep in a pile on a fluffy round bed I keep in the café just for them.

They look so cozy and content in that pile I wish I could join them for a nap. It sounds like one of them is snoring, but I'm not sure which.

In case you're wondering, the café isn't full of pet hair because of a spell I designed that keeps them from losing any fur inside the café walls. My house, however, is another matter. Who knew these petite five-pound rabbits could continuously produce so much hair? Or make that *hare*, I laugh to myself.

"You guys are useless," I tell the still-sleeping animals. "I think I'll go talk to Serenity. I bet she'll have a good idea."

"I'll walk out with you boss. I'm not getting anywhere on this recipe either," Damien tells me.

He waves goodbye as he heads to the parking lot while I head in the opposite direction to the candy shop.

Chapter 12

As I walk over to Serenity's shop, I crave one of her enchanted hot chocolate bombs. The one that swirls glittering rainbow colors as it melts in the heavy glass mug. I'll talk her into joining me so we can sip the chocolatey goodness while we discuss what I can do next to solve this mystery.

I push open the door, smiling at the recording that plays the Monster Mash song to let her know a customer has entered. I'm surprised she isn't at the front counter like she normally is. Perhaps she's in the back.

"Hey, Serenity! It's me, Charlotte!" I call out. More silence. "Serenity?" I don't want to startle her. Maybe she's in the bathroom. "Serenity?" I whisper as I step softly toward the back of her store. My whisper spirals into a scream when I see her lying on the ground in the storage room.

"Serenity!" I cry, racing to her side while dropping to my knees. I put my fingers on her neck. Phew! There's a pulse. It's faint, but at least she's alive. I pull my phone from my pocket to dial 911.

"I just found Serenity passed out in her shop! Please help! It's Serenity's Sweets!" I shout into the phone. My heart races, my voice sounds ragged and harsh.

"Is she injured?" the operator asks.

"I don't know! I can't tell. There's no blood!"

"Is she sick?"

"I'm telling you, I don't know! Just send an ambulance!" I beg.

While talking to the operator, I see a piece of paper on the ground next to Serenity's head. It's light pink, with neatly formed letters written with thick black marker.

DROP OUT OF THE RACE AND THE INVESTIGATION OR BODIES WILL FALL.

For a moment, I nearly forget about Serenity as I stare at the note in shock. This has to be for me, right? Not to sound self-absorbed, but who else could it be? Certainly not Serenity.

"Step away from the body!" I hear a familiar voice command.

Not again. I drop the note as I back away from Serenity. I twist on my heel to face Detective Thomas.

"Please! You have to help. Something is wrong with my friend!" I beg her.

"I heard the 911 call," she tells me while kneeling to check for a pulse, yet never taking her eyes or gun off me. "The ambulance is here," she says as we hear the sirens stop in front of the shop. Several seconds later, a pair of Crested Peaks EMTs enter the store.

"We're in the back!" Detective Thomas shouts. When the paramedics enter the back room, they're surprised to see me standing there with my hands in the air, Detective Thomas pointing her gun at me.

"Hurry up!" she barks, pointing at Serenity.

They quickly recover from their shock, rushing to help her.

"What is this?" the detective asks, picking up the note I just dropped. She reads it and frowns. "Care to explain?"

"I don't know where that came from," I insist.

"I just saw you holding it."

"I found it when I was checking on Serenity." I point at the ground where I found the note.

"What were you doing back here? This isn't your shop," she says.

"I stopped in the store to talk to my friend, but when she wasn't out front, I came back here looking for her."

"What were you here to talk about?" she asks. My hesitation is apparent. I can't tell the detective I came to discuss the investigation. Why am I such a lousy liar? "Word has it you've been all over town investigating Herb Appleton's murder."

I shrug. "She's a friend. I stopped in to say hello."

The detective glares at me. Why won't she believe me?

"I'll ask you again. Where did the note come from?"

"I don't know." I shake my head vigorously. "I assume whoever did this to her left it for me to find."

"How do you know someone did something to her? Why would they leave a note for *you*?"

"Oh, well, I guess I don't know for sure. But obviously, something happened here!"

"You know what I think?" she crooks her head at me.

Uh oh. Here it comes.

"I think your so-called friend here knows the truth about Herb's death, so you had to keep her quiet."

"What?" I shriek. "You're out of your mind!"

"Whose fingerprints will I find on the note?" she asks. "Aside from yours?"

She's baiting me. "Certainly not mine!" I insist right before I remember picking it up. "Oh, except..." Ugh. Why did I touch that? How was I supposed to know? Detective Thomas puts the note in an evidence bag with far more drama than I think is necessary. "Mmmm hmmm," is all she says.

"Is she going to be okay?" I asked the paramedics as they wheel the gurney out of the back room.

"Get back!" Detective Thomas pushes me away from Serenity.

I'm so close to really freaking out here. I don't know what happened to Serenity, and Detective Thomas looks like she's ready to toss me in jail and throw away the key.

"Keep me updated," she tells them while they load Serenity into the back of the ambulance.

I open my mouth to tell them *me too*, but the icy glare from Detective Thomas shuts me up.

"I'm watching every move you make," she says, waving the note in my face.

"Why would I write a note like that, attack my friend, and then call the ambulance?" I ask a little more sharply than I mean to. She just gets to me.

"You did it on purpose to throw us off," she suggests.

There's no winning with this woman. We glare at each other while another police car pulls up.

"You need to leave this area so we can investigate. Don't go very far in case I have questions."

"I'm right next door." I tell her.

"Isn't that convenient?" she responds.

I flip the sign to *Closed*. "Could you at least make sure no one steals anything?" I ask.

"We'll do our best," she sneers.

Yeah, I get it. She thinks I attacked Serenity, so now it's silly that I'm worried about her shop.

I step out the door and nearly get run over by Damien. "Boss! Are you okay? What happened?"

"What are you doing here? I sent you home for the night," I scold him.

"I forgot my laptop and came back to get it. I saw your car in the parking lot and knew you must still be here. But when I couldn't find you, I got worried. When I heard the sirens, I ran over here."

Just as I'm about to tell him what happened, Miranda hurries over from across the street while a crowd gathers to see what all the fuss is about. "What's going on?" she asks.

"We should go inside," I tell them. I don't want to explain in front of everyone.

Meanwhile, Damien checks me over.

"I didn't get hurt," I tell him, swatting his hand away.

"I'm just checking!" he exclaims as we shuffle into the café.

"All right, spill!" Miranda tells me, planting her feet and crossing her arms over her chest. Maybe she should consider police work over owning a coffee shop.

I take a deep breath, trying to overcome my urge to collapse. "I went next door to discuss the case with Serenity. I thought she might have an idea about what to do next. But I found her lying on the ground, passed out. There was a note beside her that read *drop out of the race and the investigation or bodies will fall.*"

Damien gasps. "Was the note meant for you?"

"It would have to be, wouldn't it?" I tell them, my voice and my legs still shaky from the trauma of finding my friend on the floor.

"Well, where is it?" Miranda asks.

"Detective Thomas took it as evidence," I sigh.

"Please tell me you didn't touch it," Miranda says.

"Wellll..."

"You touched it?" Damien cries.

"Of course! I picked it up to read it!" I tell them. "I wasn't thinking about fingerprints. My friend was lying motionless on the ground. That's what I was thinking about!"

"OK, calm down, we get it," Miranda says. "What now?"

"We have to find out what happened to Serenity," I insist.

"Do you know anything at all about that?"

I shake my head. "Detective Thomas wouldn't let the paramedics say anything in front of me. I'm terrified something horrible has happened to her!"

"We'll figure out a way to get an update," Damien assures me.

"Who could do such a thing?" I cry. "What if she dies? What if the same person framing me for Herb's murder wants to kill Serenity and frame me for that, too?"

Damien shakes his head. "I don't like this at all. One of us could be next," he says, pointing at each of us.

I nod my head. "I don't want anyone else getting hurt. I'm dropping out of the race. It isn't worth it. I don't need to be mayor. Maybe they can start the process all over again with new candidates," I suggest hopefully.

"No! You aren't dropping out. Crested Peaks needs you," Miranda insists.

"But what if my friends are in danger? It could be either of you. What if Damien's family is in danger? It was one thing to kill Herb, given the number of people who had issues with him, but what if they're after my friends now? I can't take that risk. I'm dropping out."

Chapter 13

By the next day, Damien and Miranda talk me out of withdrawing from the mayoral race. For now, anyway.

Drew called late last night after speaking with his contact at the hospital. The doctors were shocked to discover that Serenity inhaled a minuscule amount of Strychnine.

Thankfully, I found her just in time, so she'll be okay. They say it would have been too late if I'd discovered her even 30 minutes later. I shudder just thinking about it.

His contact also told him that when Detective Thomas questioned Serenity and said I was a suspect, she went berserk. They even had to ask the detective to leave.

She kept shouting that there was no way her friend Charlotte tried to kill her and, most assuredly, didn't kill Herb Appleton.

She told them that someone had left a yellow rose on the countertop of the shop. She wondered why it was there, then picked it up and smelled it, of course, like anyone would do.

After that, she doesn't remember a thing. She's just glad that no one else accidentally picked it up. The police swear there was no rose on the counter. Whoever tried to kill her must have waited until she collapsed, took the rose, and then left the note beside her.

I'm relieved when I remember that I was with Damien until the moment I walked over to Serenity's shop, so I have a solid alibi. I shouldn't even need an alibi, but I'm glad I have it nonetheless.

After a hectic morning rush, Damien insists I take a break to hang out with Miranda in the coffee shop before she closes it for their afternoon staff retreat to the miniature golf course. She's treating everyone to a fun afternoon before the snow flies and the skiers keep them extra busy throughout the winter.

While I wait for her to make my pumpkin spice chai with an extra dash of cinnamon, I can't help but stare at two women chatting away at a table nearby. They look vaguely familiar, yet I can't quite place them.

One of them is complaining bitterly about her boss. From the way she's talking, this boss sounds like a real pain. When I hear her say the name Tilly, I almost gasp out loud. Then I move closer to hear them better.

When Miranda places my chai next to the cash register, I put my finger over my lips to keep her quiet. She gives me her *oh dear, what are you up to now* look. I gesture ever so slightly with my head at the pair of women.

"Here I was all set to meet up with that hot guy I met at the dry cleaner in Aspen, but oh no, her highness insisted that I wear that ridiculous cat woman costume so I could fill in for her at the charity event while she galavanted off to who knows where in secret!"

My mouth drops as I stare at Miranda in shock. They aren't exactly whispering, so I know she heard it too. Tilly lied about where she was when Herb was killed! Now I remember where I saw the woman who's doing most of the complaining. She's Tilly's assistant.

That means Tilly wasn't at the charity event like she told us. She snuck off to kill Herb instead! I knew there was something fishy about her story right from the beginning.

I run back across the street to the cafe with Miranda chasing me. My chai stays on the countertop, forgotten.

I burst through the front door of Marcall's. "You guys. You're never going to believe this!" I pant to a surprised Damien and Aranya, along with a startled customer, eating lunch in the corner.

When Miranda pushes through the door behind me, she nearly runs into me. No doubt the customer in the corner is wondering if this chaos is common here.

"Tilly's assistant is in the coffee shop right now complaining about how she had to fill in for her boss at the charity event on Halloween!"

Damien breaks in. "How can that be? Tilly sent us the video proving she was there in the cat woman costume--" Before he finishes, his mouth falls open as he realizes what he just said. "Her assistant wore the costume and pretended to be Tilly?"

"Yes!" I shout, practically jumping up and down. I'm so excited. "Tilly made her assistant take her place at the party so she could come here to kill Herb! It makes perfect sense!"

"But how did she get the hatchet from your garage? How would she know where you live? Besides, she'd have to break in without you knowing it?" Aranya asks.

"Who cares? We can figure it out later! This has to be it!" I'm frustrated that they aren't as excited as I am. Why does Aranya have to ask so many questions?

Damien crooks his head. "I'm with Aranya on this one. It's a gigantic leap from Tilly lying to us to breaking into your garage and framing you. In addition to attacking Serenity."

"He has a point," Miranda adds.

"Not you too!" I complain.

"You know I want to catch whoever did this as much as you, and while I understand that Tilly clearly had a motive to kill Herb--"

"--and publicly threatened to kill him!" I remind her.

She nods her head. "Yes, I remember that. We know she lied to us, but we still don't know why she would want to frame you."

"Because she doesn't want to get caught!" I insist. Why can't they see this the way I do?

"Do you think your desperation to find the killer lets you see things that aren't there?" Aranya asks.

"Fine!" I snap. "You can all believe whatever you want. I'm going to track down Tilly right now and confront her. When she confesses to killing Herb and attacking Serenity to scare me into dropping out of the race and investigating Herb's murder, you'll all wish you'd believed me to begin with."

I stomp out the door, get in my car, and head straight for the lake behind the Hotel Glacier. That's where the assistant mentioned they were filming.

"Excuse me," I ask someone with a clipboard, hoping he can help me. "Do you know where I can find Tilly Rock?"

He wordlessly points to a trailer with a door that says "Tilly" in sparkling letters. Security around here is a bit lax, if you ask me, which is a good thing in this case.

I pound on her door. "Tilly! It's Charlotte Duffin. I need to speak with you!"

Tilly throws open the door. "Sakes alive, child; where's the earthquake?"

"You lied to me!" I scowl at her.

"Okayyyyy. Why don't you come in?"

She ushers me inside her lavish trailer. I look around. Numerous People's Choice awards line the shelves. Who knew you could win awards for reality tv? There are fresh, fragrant flowers in thick glass vases spread throughout.

A colorful display of various kinds of cheese and meats are arranged on a tray on the coffee table. An uncorked champagne bottle rests in an ice bucket nearby. Tilly leads quite the life. Too bad for her, it's all about to come crashing down.

"You need to explain this to me. When did I lie to you? I barely know you."

"You said you were at a charity event in Aspen when Herb was killed."

"That's right. I sent you a video clip of me at the fundraiser."

Is it me, or is she sweating a little? "Where you attended in costume."

She hesitates. "Yes. What is this all about?"

"I just overheard your assistant telling a friend that you forced her to wear the costume and go to the event, so you didn't have to. I think you came to Crested Peaks, broke into my garage, stole my hatchet, and killed Herb instead. Then you tried to kill my friend Serenity to scare me into dropping out of the race."

When she bursts into laughter, I'm stunned. How could she think this is funny? She must be crazy. That would explain a lot.

"Girl, I don't have the faintest idea of what you're talking about. For starters, I don't even know where you live. How could I break into your garage and steal your hatchet? Who is this Serenity person I supposedly tried to kill?"

When she sees me looking shocked at her outburst, she throws her hands over her face, roaring with laughter.

My cheeks get hot. When the others pointed that out in the cafe, it sounded like they were just making up excuses. But when she says it, it's painfully real.

"Well, then you paid someone!"

"Oh, sweetie. If I really wanted to kill Herb, I could have run him down in my car long ago. But I guess I can tell you the truth, now that it's practically a done deal. You have to promise you won't tell anyone until they publicly announce it."

"What's practically a done deal?" I ask, as I feel my answer to Herb's murder slipping away.

"I asked Andrea to fill in for me at the party on Halloween night because I was negotiating with an executive from another network. She's almost the same size and build, so I knew she would look like me in that costume. I'm leaving Bored Rich Housewives and getting my own talk show. That's where I was on Halloween. It all had to be top secret. If the other network rejected me, I didn't want to jeopardize my role on Bored Rich Housewives."

"Do you have proof you met with the other network?" My solution is sinking fast, but I'm not going down without a fight.

She chuckles. "Sure, I can get you proof if you want, but I assure you, I'm not your killer."

I leave Tilly's trailer with the personal cell phone number of the network executive who's giving her the talk show. As much as I want him to tell me she's lying and that he's never even heard of her, I know in my heart it's over.

Tilly didn't kill Herb, so I'm down to either Frank or Ted. It also means time is running out for me to figure out which of them did it.

Chapter 14

While returning to the cafe after talking with Tilly, I scold myself. What was I thinking? I wanted to solve this case and clear my name so badly that I'm willing to convince myself of anything, I guess.

Sure, it was evident that Tilly was happy Herb was dead, yet painfully apparent she would have had to go to extremes to frame me for it and kill Serenity in the process.

The same goes for Ted if I'm being perfectly honest with myself. His issue was with Herb, not with me. He likes me!

Which leaves Frank. Whether he admits it or not, he must have a problem with Herb because of what went on between Herb and his wife.

Plus, he definitely doesn't want me as mayor. As far as Frank is concerned, it's personal with Herb and business with me, which is a lot of motive. I think he's the only suspect who didn't publicly threaten to kill Herb.

That's it. I have to talk to Frank again. His office address was on a flyer we picked up when we spoke with him at the seminar at the community center, so I know exactly where it is.

When I arrive, I'm dismayed there aren't any available parking spots nearby. I drive around the block, searching for another place that might be at least somewhat close, when I see them. I don't realize it's them at first, but something about their body language makes me look twice.

Then I'm so busy staring that I nearly run into the car in front of me, stopped at the stop sign. Frank Goodman and Charles Hardy, my parents' friend, are in the parking lot, and they appear to be arguing.

Frank is making wild gestures with his hands, while Charles glares at him, his hands planted on his waist as he leans in with a menacing look.

"What on earth?" I whisper to myself. How do those two know each other? I'm so engrossed in watching them that I forget I'm still stopped in the middle of the road.

The driver behind me finally lays on his horn, startling me from my trance. Unfortunately, the blare of the horn also draws Frank and Charles' attention as they swing around to see what the noise is. I duck down so they can't see me while the driver behind me continues honking.

I peek above the dashboard just enough so I can move forward while continuing to watch Frank and Charles. They're still looking in my direction, too. I realize how ridiculous I must look driving along, like I'm three feet tall and can barely see over the dashboard.

I go left at the stop sign, but when I look over again to see what they're doing, they're gone. I sit up straight in the car and look every-where. There's no sign of them.

"Shoot!" I smack my hand on the steering wheel. I have to know what they were doing. How do they know each other? What if they're in this together?

What if Frank decided he needed help to get rid of Herb and me? Who better than one of my parents' old felon friends? I knew that guy was up to no good when he showed up at the cafe blathering on about

Gran's big…. Holy cow, that's it. Charles knows where I live, and if anybody would know how to break into someone's garage, it would be him!

I can't believe this. This has to be the answer. Why didn't I think of this before?

I quickly circle the block several times, desperately searching for them, but there's no sign. What I do find is a newly opened parking spot that I slip into.

I ponder my options. I should tell someone, but who? I don't want to get Drew in trouble. For a second, I even consider calling Detective Thomas, but she won't believe me. Plus, I'd have to admit that I'm investigating this case.

I'll call Miranda. She'll know what to do. I groan when it goes straight to voicemail. "Hi, this is Miranda. I'm unavailable today because I'm on a retreat with my staff. Leave a message, and I'll get back to you this evening."

Argh! Double rats! I already forgot her store is closed this afternoon for her staff retreat. It's up to me to confront Frank and, hopefully, even Chuck. It's not like I've never done it before. I lock the car and head up to his office on the third floor.

It's a quiet, non-descript office. Nothing fancy about it. There's a small refrigerator along the wall with a glass door, so visitors can see the different types of beverages available. A colorful sign next to it reads "Please take one!"

There's a large round table in the middle of the waiting area with a bowl full of snack sized bags of chips, cookies, and crackers. Next to that is a large vase full of fresh roses which I can smell as I walk by. I approach the receptionist, who is engrossed in a wild game of Candy Crush.

"Can I help you?" she asks.

"Hi, I have an appointment with Frank. I'd like to talk to him about getting a loan for a condo."

"He's not in this afternoon. I'll have to take a message. Did you say you had an appointment?"

"Yes." I lie.

She glances down at an empty calendar. "I don't have anyone down for an appointment."

"Oh. I see. Well, he must have forgotten."

"Can I get your name?" she asks.

"Uh, no, that's okay. I'll talk to him later."

"Suit yourself." She shrugs and goes back to playing with her phone.

I punch the button for the elevator and ride down, growing increasingly frustrated.

Why is this always so hard? I know it was Frank and Charles. But now I have to find them. I drive back to Marcall's, my mind awhirl with what to do next.

When I get back to the cafe, it's late in the afternoon, almost closing time. I explain everything that just happened to Damien .

"That's it, boss. You have to call Detective Thomas and tell her what you know."

I grimace. "I was thinking the same thing. But what if she doesn't believe me?"

"I still think you should try. If Frank and Charles stole the hatchet from your garage to frame you, *then* killed Herb, and *then* tried to kill Serenity, that makes them incredibly dangerous. They'll obviously stop at nothing to get at you. You need real help right now."

"I suppose you're right," I sigh. I look over at Miranda's shop again. "Did Miranda say when she'd be back from her retreat?"

"I'm not sure. I think it was sometime this evening," he tells me.

"Okay, well, you can take off if you want. I doubt we'll get a big rush in the next 20 minutes. Anybody we do get, I'm sure I can handle."

"You're not just sending me home because you think I'm going to keep nagging you to call Detective Thomas, are you?"

I laugh. "No, I'm sure you're right. I should call her. Are the boys in the back room?"

"No, last I checked, they were heading out for their usual afternoon visit to the Five Dachshund Bakery for fresh cookies."

"Okay, I'll wait here for them. I'll also call Detective Thomas," I cut him off before he can nag me about it again.

"Okie dokie! Call me if you need anything!" he says on his way out the door.

I pace the dining room of Marcall's alone, mulling over how Frank and Charles could be connected. I'm still baffled how they know each other, but given that Charles knows where I live, Frank could have hired him to steal the hatchet from my house.

I bet that day Charles showed up here, he did it just to taunt me. That was a mistake. I wouldn't have realized who he was this afternoon if he hadn't come here before. I finally decide Damien is right. I'll call Detective Thomas to tell her what I saw today.

I call the front desk of the police department, but she's out. Why isn't anybody answering their phone today?

I'm in the middle of leaving a message for her when Marshall, Marcus, and Stumpy burst through the front door, shouting, "Hey, lady! The coffee shop is on fire!"

Chapter 15

I've never seen the expressions that are on their faces right now. Terror has replaced their usual sauciness. I've also never seen Stumpy move that fast.

"What's going on?" I ask, my pulse quickening.

"The coffee shop is on fire!" Marshall shouts again.

I tell them they better not be joking while secretly hoping they are. I peer across the street, but I see nothing. No fire anyway.

"Go!" Marshall and Marcus shout in stereo.

"You wait here!" I jab my finger at them while they nod their heads. Now I know it's serious because they never do what I tell them.

I run out the door toward the coffee shop, but when I smell smoke, I pull my phone from my apron pocket and shout at the operator that there is a fire in Bean Around a Bit.

I press my face against the front window. The rabbits were right. The coffee shop is on fire! I'm at least somewhat relieved when I remember it was closed for the retreat.

I pray no one is in there, but then I see it. A body. Oh, please let them be alive. The thick black smoke makes it surprisingly dark inside, but as my eyes adjust, it's unmistakable. The short body with spiky orange and purple hair is Miranda.

"Help!" I scream. Why are the sidewalks suddenly so empty this afternoon? They're never empty! Where is everyone? I hear the sirens, but they're still so far off. "Hurry!" I shout, even though no one is listening. Why is that fire truck taking so long?

The fire grows right in front of my eyes. Now the smoke is so thick I can't see Miranda anymore. What if the ceiling caves in before the fire department arrives? I have to do something. Calm down, I tell myself. You've used witchcraft on fire before.

Think, Charlotte, think! I wrench open the door and instantly choke. I try using a spell to thin the smoke, but it only helps a little. Concentrating and using magic while I'm in a hurry and panicking is more complicated than I anticipated.

"Miranda!" I call out, then cough again. I can't see anything. I shift my focus to illuminating the cafe so there's some light. There she is! I drop to my hands and knees, crawling to her as fast as I can. When I'm at her side, I try to pick her up. How can someone so little be so heavy?

"Light as a feather!" I chant several times, making it easier for me to pick her up. I grip my hands under her arms while dragging her toward the door. It's so hard to concentrate all at once on everything. I'm trying to tame the fire, alleviate the smoke, and keep the shop illuminated, all while making Miranda lighter.

I can only hold out for a few more seconds. I struggle to the front door; using a final magical burst of energy, I fling it open and collapse outside. I continue to choke and gasp for air. Miranda has fallen on top of me, she suddenly feels heavy again.

Thankfully, the Crested Peaks Fire Department has arrived. Fire-fighters spill out of the truck, with the paramedics right behind them. It's the same paramedics who found me with Serenity. They look surprised to see me. I want to explain, but I can't talk. Every time I try, I suffer through another fit of painful coughing.

I swear I'll never take being able to breathe for granted again. I watch the firefighters preparing to battle the fire as I struggle to push away the paramedic trying to put an oxygen mask on my face.

"I can help them," I insist.

"They've got it, ma'am. Let us help you."

"No, you don't understand," I continue to push him away. I want to help them with my magic, but I can't do it with him fussing over me like this.

I watch the EMTs load Miranda into an ambulance while I cry out, "Will she be okay? Can you help her?" I beg them right before another coughing fit.

"We'll do everything we can, ma'am. Right now, you need to calm down."

As I inhale deeply through the oxygen mask, Drew races up in an unmarked patrol car, leaving it in the middle of the street. He runs to me, his face full of worry.

"Char! What happened here? Are you okay?"

"She's fighting our medical help, Detective," they tell him.

"I can take it from here," he says. "I'll let you know if we need help."

The paramedic is skeptical. But when he sees I'm determined, he gives up and backs away.

"Are you all right? Are you burned anywhere?" he asks.

I shake my head no while pulling off the oxygen mask. "I'm not burned. I have to help the firefighters with magic!"

"The fire is almost out, Char. Right now, you need to calm down and let us help you. Do you know how this started? Was anyone else in there?"

I pull the mask off again. It's getting a little easier to breathe. "Marshall, Marcus, and Stumpy saw it and ran to get me."

"Are you serious? Are *they* okay?" he says, looking around in a panic

"I told them to wait in the café while I checked everything out. I ran over, and I could see the fire inside the shop. Then I saw Miranda passed out on the floor."

"You went in there by yourself?" Drew asks, horrified.

"I used magic," I explain.

"Charlotte Duffin, you could have been killed!" he scolds me.

"It was taking too long for the fire department to arrive," I point out.

Drew rakes his hand down his face, groaning in frustration.

"Is Miranda going to be okay? This is my fault!" I sob.

"How is it your fault?" he asks.

"They warned me to drop out of the race and stop investigating Herb's death. If only I had listened, to begin with, we wouldn't be in this mess."

"Do you think you know who did it?" Drew asks.

I nod my head sorrowfully.

"Seriously?"

I pull the note out of my pocket that I found on Miranda. It's written on the same pink paper with the same black marker and the same ominous warning as the other one.

DROP OUT OF THE RACE AND THE INVESTIGATION OR BODIES WILL FALL.

"Where did you get this?" he asks, snatching it from my hand.

"It was in Miranda's shirt pocket," I explain.

"You took it?"

"I had to make sure it didn't get lost," I tell him.

"You're tampering with evidence!" he scolds.

"But I have something to tell you!" I insist.

"Well, well, well, isn't this cozy?" Detective Thomas says.

I groan and roll my eyes. Drew stands up so he can stare down at her. If he was hoping to intimidate her, I think he's out of luck. She isn't swaying.

"What do you have in your hand, Detective?" she asks.

"It's a note that was on the victim," he explains, handing it to her.

"Why do you have it? You know you're not allowed on this case," she snaps.

"When Ms. Duffin risked her own life to save the victim, the note attached to the victim accidentally stuck to Ms. Duffin. I took it from her to place it in police custody. I may not be allowed on this case, but I'm still a detective, and I still outrank *you*, Detective. See that you properly catalog the evidence."

Detective Thomas pinches her lips while staring up at him. "Fine!" she grumbles, pulling an evidence bag from her jacket pocket. "I still need to question Ms. Duffin. If you don't mind, I'd like you to wait elsewhere."

Drew nods curtly. "I'll be right over here if you need anything."

I smile up at him. I can't believe Drew just lied to a fellow detective. He never lies. I've made such a mess. Drew gets pulled from a case because of me, Serenity gets poisoned, and Miranda could die. My stomach roils at the thought.

I should have dropped out of the stupid race a long time ago. Scratch that; I should never have run in the first place. Instead, I get the grandiose idea that I, of all people, could become mayor of Crested Peaks.

"I wish I could say I'm surprised to see you here, but by now, I'm not. Considering I catch you at every crime scene in town, I'm certain it's just a matter of time before I get solid evidence to arrest you," she tells me.

"Do you have questions for me or just threats?" I ask. I've run out of patience with this lady.

"You are in no position to sass me, Ms. Duffin."

"Did you get my message?" I ask.

"Yes, the desk sergeant let me know you called. But you didn't say why you were calling. I assume it was to confess to starting the fire?"

"What? No!"

"Then why did you call?"

"I called to tell you I saw Frank Goodman and Charles Hardy arguing this afternoon."

"I should care about this?"

"Yes!" I exclaim.

"Why?"

"Because Herb Appleton had an affair with Frank's wife, and Frank didn't like the policy changes I've proposed for Crested Peaks if I'm elected mayor."

"Excuse me?" she says.

That didn't sound as dramatic and final as I was hoping. "Charles Hardy is an old friend of my parents. I know that he's up to no good."

"What is your point to all of this?"

"I'm sure they broke into my garage, stole my hatchet, killed Herb, and framed me for it. Then they tried to kill Serenity, and now Miranda, just to keep me from becoming mayor."

I swear, for a moment, she's about to laugh. "That's a mighty tall tale for someone who was told repeatedly to stay out of this investigation. Now, why don't you tell me how you discovered the fire? Assuming you'll deny setting it yourself. What were you doing inside? The paramedics told me you were the one who dragged Miranda out.

How did you know she was in there if you didn't start it? They told me the shop was closed for the afternoon."

I really want to give her a good pinch. Instead, I explain everything, minus the part where two rabbits and a cat told me the shop was on fire. Instead, I opt to tell her I smelled smoke.

"So, you're claiming that you didn't start the fire?"

"What reason would I have to set my best friend's shop on fire?"

"The same reason you poisoned Serenity. Your best friend knows you killed Herb Appleton, so you have to get rid of her. Maybe she helped you kill him; now she feels guilty about it and wants to go to the police."

"I've had enough of this." I struggle to get to my feet to show this detective what I really think of her.

"I think our time here is done!" Drew says as he runs back to grab me by the arm, escorting me in the opposite direction.

"I was just getting started!" I tell him, trying to wriggle away.

"I can see that," he says.

"You can call her if you have any more questions, Detective," he tells her.

"What are you doing?" I hiss.

"You're in enough trouble already," he hisses back. "You don't need any more on your plate."

"Fine, I guess you're right," I grumble as I let him lead me away. He helps me collect my things at the café, then drives me, Marshall, Marcus, and Stumpy home.

I explain everything I saw with Frank and Charles and what I think they did to kill Herb, frame me, and attempt to kill Serenity and Miranda.

"You must admit that's a big stretch, Char."

"I don't see it that way!" I protest. "Besides, it makes the most sense!"

"Whatever you do, promise me you'll be careful. I'm still barred from working on this case, but I'll see what I can do from the sidelines. I'll talk to Detective Thomas, and maybe she'll at least look into it, okay? I'll check on you tonight after my shift is done. In the meantime, if you need anything, call me."

I nod reluctantly. "I don't plan to leave this house for a long time."

He tilts his head at me. "Promise me you won't investigate this anymore. Someone is trying to kill the people you know, and I don't want you to be next, okay?"

"I hear you," I tell him.

After he finally leaves, I call the county Elections Division. Of course, no one there answers either. It's late Friday afternoon, so I'm sure I won't hear anything until Monday morning if I'm lucky.

I'm saddened thinking of the election on Tuesday and how supportive everyone was, and how hard we worked, but it's for the best.

"Hi, this is Charlotte Duffin. I'm calling to see what I need to do to officially drop out of the mayoral race. I know this is last minute, but it's the safest thing to do. You can start over fresh with two candidates and hold a special election next month. I don't know how any of this works, but if you could call me back and let me know if I need to submit any paperwork or sign something, that would be great. Thanks."

I hang up and sigh. I've failed. I'm heartbroken.

Chapter 16

Next, I text Damien and Aranya to tell them I won't be in tomorrow, and if they want to take the day off, I'm fine with closing the cafe.

I'm not sure it's appropriate for us to be open anyway, considering Miranda and Serenity were nearly killed in the same week. Wouldn't it be disrespectful to keep pretending it is business as usual?

I let them know I dropped out of the race as well. They are so thoughtful and assure me they understand, which almost makes me feel worse.

For some weird reason, I think I'd feel better if they were mad. If they complained about how much work they had put into my campaign, I could at least feel sorry for myself.

The following morning, I compose a statement to all my volunteers and supporters, letting them know that while I deeply appreciate their support, it's in the best interest for everyone involved if I leave the race. I explain that I think they can choose new and better candidates, and I'm confident the county will hold a special election soon.

I'll make the formal announcement on Monday after I talk to the Elections Division about what I need to do to drop out officially.

Meanwhile, with the weekend off, I'll tackle some sorely needed yard work that I've been neglecting for months. The yard is a mess, and there are leaves and weeds everywhere.

I use a rake to hack away at the dead leaves and tangled weeds. It's good to work hard and clear my head. My next-door neighbor Rich stops by while I work.

"Hey there, Rich," I tell him.

"Hey, Charlotte. I heard about what happened at Bean Around A Bit yesterday. They're saying you saved Miranda from the fire?"

News travels so fast in this small town. I think I'd be used to it by now, but I still get surprised.

I want to tell Rich that it was my fault Miranda's life was in danger in the first place and that he shouldn't praise me for saving her, but I don't. I just nod my head.

"She'll be okay, right?" he asks.

"Her boyfriend Miles called this morning. Thankfully, she only suffered some minor smoke inhalation and should be out of the hospital by tomorrow."

"Oh, that's good to hear," he says.

I nod my head again.

"Hey, I keep forgetting to tell you I was the one who closed your garage door on Halloween."

"Come again?" I ask. Why was my neighbor in my garage?

"You forgot to close the garage door after you left for work. I assumed you didn't want it left open all day like that."

"I left the door open?"

"I guess so. I'm sure you were distracted with the big holiday and the debate that night. Although, you may want to check on your garage door clicker. The battery could be getting low. Maybe you pushed it, but it didn't close the door. Either way, you should replace the battery. I used the keypad code you gave me for emergencies to close it. I keep meaning to tell you, but I haven't seen you around."

"Do you remember what time you closed it?" I ask. My mind is abuzz with explanations right now.

"I think it was around 9 AM or so. I know you leave for work super early, so, unfortunately, it was open for several hours before I noticed it. I hope nothing got stolen."

"Oh, thanks, yeah, everything is fine," I tell him. I guess that answers how Frank and Charles stole my hatchet. They didn't even have to break in. They walked in through the wide-open garage door and walked out with none of us the wiser.

So that was my fault too. I was sure delusional for thinking I'd grown up enough to be mayor of Crested Peaks.

"I have to go to the grocery store now, but I wanted to double-check everything was okay with you after the fire," Rich says.

"I'm fine. Thank you. Also, thank you for closing the door on Halloween."

"Sure, no problem." He waves as he walks off. "You can't be too careful these days. You never know who might walk in and take something."

No kidding. So that's that. But what do I do with it? Detective Thomas doesn't believe me, and Drew will just tell me I have to talk to her about it anyway.

Right now, I need to lie low, and once Frank and Charles find out I dropped out of the race, they'll realize I'm no longer a threat. I'll trust the police to do their job like I'm supposed to. Let Detective Thomas solve this case. That's what she wanted all along, anyway.

I'm grateful that Miranda and Serenity will be okay, but it was too close for comfort. I can't keep putting my friends in danger. I don't know what it is about this town, but I swear if it isn't me getting shot at or nearly blown up, it's one of my friends. It's amazing anyone still speaks to me.

I grab a shovel from the hook on the garage wall and hike out to the backyard to dig up some rose bushes I want to transplant. When I hear rustling in the trees, I call out. "Rich, is that you? I swear I'm fine. You don't have to keep checking on me."

"Good to know you're fine because you won't be soon," Charles Hardy says.

"What are you doing here?" I'm so startled I drop my shovel. I reach for my phone to call the police, but it isn't in my pocket. I suddenly remember leaving it on the front porch.

"When I was at your cafe the other day, I failed to mention that your parents owe me money."

"You've got to be joking." I scowl at him.

"I never joke about money."

"I don't care what my parents supposedly owe you. You better leave right now."

I'm not wasting any time on this loser. He tried to kill two of my friends and killed Herb. Now he's here, threatening me. I'll hex him and call the cops.

"Or what?" he says. "You'll hex me?"

"You bet I will!" I snarl.

"You forget I'm a wizard like your parents."

Before I can react, there's a flash of light, and I get thrown to the ground with such force that the wind is knocked out of me. I struggle to get up, but I can't move. I'm frozen. It's like I have invisible ropes binding my hands and feet.

He laughs at my struggle. "It's called a freezing spell, you fool. You should have asked your granny to teach you."

"What do you want?" I demand, while running through every counterspell I can think of in my mind. Unfortunately, I come up empty.

"Our mutual friend Frank hired me to scare you into dropping out of the race. From the rumors I'm hearing, it worked."

I glare at him while he laughs again.

"Before I leave town, though, I think I'll just help myself to what your family owes me."

"What makes you think I'll give you a darn thing?" I growl.

"Give it. Take it. It's all the same to me. You can't move, so I'll just go through your house and collect some things I think are valuable. Especially those magical rabbits of yours. I bet they'd fetch a high price on the black magic market."

He cackles when he sees the look of surprise and then sheer terror on my face.

"You forget I knew your family back in the day. You may not tell anyone about the talking rabbits these days, but I remember them well. Weird little creatures following your grandma everywhere. They've been around for decades. They're obviously not normal rabbits. I bet a lab would pay top dollar to dissect and study them."

I struggle to overcome his magic, but he's too powerful. I swear if he touches those rabbits, I'll hunt him down to the ends of the earth and make him pay.

"There's a wall safe in the bedroom with cash. You can have it all," I tell him.

"Aww, look at you, offering me cash. Like you're in any position to negotiate with me. Maybe I'll grab that stupid crippled cat while I'm at it. Just to sweeten the pot for my buyers. I bet he talks too, doesn't he?"

I narrow my eyes at him. "Fine. But don't forget to smile," I tell him.

"What?"

"Smile for the nice detective."

"What are you talking about?" He whirls around to see what I'm staring at behind him. Detective Thomas swings the shovel I was using a few minutes ago to clock him in the face so hard she breaks his nose and knocks him out cold.

The moment he's unconscious, it breaks the spell, and I'm free. I jump to my feet, ready to smack him with the shovel myself if he so much as moves a toe.

The detective and I lock eyes while we breathe a sigh of relief.

"You believe me now?" I ask.

She nods her head, dropping the shovel. Then she cuffs him and calls for an ambulance.

"Nobody threatens animals on my watch," she says, cinching the handcuffs extra tight.

I smile. It's the first thing we've agreed on. "Amen to that, sister. But what are you doing here?" I ask.

"You're one stubborn lady; you know that?"

I nod.

"I was convinced you were guilty. Yet even I have to admit that it seemed so odd that you continued to insist you were innocent," she says.

"But don't all bad guys do that?" I ask. "I mean, I really am innocent here, but your crooks all claim they're innocent, don't they?"

"They do." She nods. "But there was just something about you. You could have run and hidden, but instead, you kept showing up to save your friends. I figured you were either completely guilty or someone was targeting you. I finally decided to give you a chance. I checked out this Frank for myself to see if there was anything to your stories. I went to his office but when I saw the huge display of fragrant yellow roses--"

I gasp while she nods her head again. I walked right by those roses and even noticed how pretty they smelled, but I didn't stop to smell them. So to speak.

"You obviously know where I'm going with this. I decided to play him and tell him we knew where the poisoned rose came from. I thought I could at least scare him a little, you know. See how he reacted."

"So, you did? Rattle him, I mean."

"Oh, I didn't just rattle him. He folded like a cheap lawn chair. The roses were just a lucky guess on my part. He hired your parents' friend Charles to scare you into dropping out of the race, which I'm sure you just found out. What he didn't hire him to do was kill Serenity or Miranda. He said he wanted Charles to scare you, not terrorize the town and burn it down."

I take a deep breath. This is just wild. I hold my finger up. "By the way, I just found out that I accidentally left my garage door open on Halloween, so that's how they were able to get my hatchet so easily."

She nods. "That makes sense. Even though Frank swears that wasn't part of the deal. But neither was killing Serenity or Miranda, so I'm sure it's just a matter of time before I break them. One of them will confess. They always do."

"Thank you," I tell her, shocking even myself. Hey, I believe in giving credit where it's due.

She's surprised. "You sound like you mean it."

"I do! You just saved my life. Along with the rabbits *and* the cat."

She leans close and whispers. "I have to ask. Are they really magic?"

I start to shrug and pretend I don't know what she's talking about, but she did save me. "My Gran won them in a poker game decades ago. You do the math."

"Wowwww," is all she says.

I don't think she believes me, but that's okay.

"At least now you can move onto election day knowing you're safe, right?

I flinch because it's still painful to think about. "I dropped out of the race yesterday."

"So, tell them you changed your mind," she insists.

"Why?"

"Because Crested Peaks needs a leader like you."

"Really?" I ask, wondering if I sound as shocked as I feel.

"Obviously, we'll never be best friends, but I've watched you this week. You're not just stubborn. It's evident that you care deeply about this town and its people. You're willing to put your life on the line when someone is in danger, whereas most would simply look the other way and tell me they don't want to get involved. Your entire livelihood and your freedom were threatened, and yet you didn't run or back down. You stood up for yourself and for this town. It's the kind of leadership that Crested Peaks needs."

When my mouth falls open in shock, she laughs. "Did I just sound like a campaign commercial?"

Chapter 17

After taking a much-needed break from the cafe this weekend, I'm eager to return to work on Monday. Serenity and Miranda were released from the hospital and are at home recuperating from their near-death experiences. Charles and Frank are in jail, so that's a relief.

Miranda told us she got a strange text from a blocked number telling her that the coffee shop was on fire. She raced back from the retreat to see if it was true and, without thinking, ran into her store when she saw smoke. When she saw the note I found in her pocket lying on the ground she picked it up to read it.

She kept telling herself to get out and call 911, but she was overcome by smoke faster than she realized was possible. After that, she woke up in the hospital.

Her insurance company assured her that they will cover most of the damage, so she has decided a bit of remodeling is in order, anyway. It was a huge relief to talk to her and Serenity this weekend. I was so thrilled to hear their voices, I cried.

They insisted that none of this was my fault, and I should stay in the race. I assured them I'd think about it.

Marshall, Marcus, and Stumpy have been sticking so close to me since Charles showed up at the house that I'm practically tripping over them. I understand they're concerned, but what happens when I fall and break my arm?

Then, just when I thought everything would be quiet for at least a little while, Ted Carter stops in for a breakfast burrito. I can only imagine the look on my face when I see him. I assumed he'd be well on his way out of town by now, after everything that happened. If it were me, I'd want a fresh start far away from here.

"It's been quite a week for this town, hasn't it?" he asks, while waiting for his order.

"That it has," I respond. There's still something off about this guy that I can't quite put my finger on. I'm hoping he doesn't stick around to talk very long. His energy has always given me the heebie-jeebies, especially so today.

He stands in front of the cash register talking for far longer than I have time for. I'm only paying attention to a part of what he's saying, anyway. He talks so fast and for so long that even if I wanted to respond, I couldn't. It's like he can talk without breathing.

"Imagine if those so-called bodyguards of Herbs hadn't taken that smoke break. He wouldn't have been alone!" he declares almost gleefully.

"Mmmm," I murmur absentmindedly. Hang on a second. What did he just say? My head snaps up, and I see it in his eyes. A flash of regret. He just couldn't leave well enough alone.

The nagging feeling I've had ever since Detective Thomas told me that Frank Goodman confessed to everything, except Herb's murder just turned into a full-blown realization.

I quickly glance down at my phone sitting on the shelf directly beneath the cash register. I hope that Ted didn't catch my whiplash-like change of focus. My hands shake as I discreetly push the redial button, hoping that he's still too distracted to notice me doing something under the counter.

"Detective Thomas here. This better be good, Duffin. Duffin? Hello?"

Then silence. I don't want to look down again and make him suspicious. I just have to hope she's still on the line listening. I need to keep him here as long as possible. The spells I might have to use on him flash through my mind.

I try to keep it casual. "Hey there, Ted; you know where I live, right?" As soon as I say it, I cringe. That was way too obvious. But it was the only thing I could think of at the moment.

He laughs. "Of course! How else would I have slipped my special plan into your mail slot?"

"Your what?" I ask. That's not what I expected him to say at all, but I'm relieved he's none the wiser.

"The special plan I developed, outlining my solution for an ideal Crested Peaks! I slipped a copy through your mail slot a few days before Halloween, but you never mentioned it. I assume that meant you just threw it out. I hope you know that really upset me. I worked hard on that and for you to just dismiss it without even looking at it is incredibly disrespectful," he lectures.

His tone changes from chatterbox to agitated. What does he mean by special plan? This guy is wackier than I thought. Maybe he had the wrong house after all.

"Are you *sure* you had the right house? I never saw it." I'm baffled by this.

"Of course, it's your house. The one with the massive wraparound porch, with flying ghosts and singing pumpkins."

He means my enchanted Halloween decorations. "Yes, that's my house." I gulp.

"I knew it!" he says triumphantly.

"But I never saw your package," I keep telling him.

Now he looks as confused as I feel.

Marshall headbutts my ankle. "It came in a plain brown envelope," he tells me.

"What? *You* saw it? Why didn't you tell me?" Ted stares at me in confusion, while I have what appears to be a pretend conversation with the rabbits.

"We were going to, but then we ate it," Marcus explains.

"You ate it?"

"We were just going to nibble around the edges, but before we knew it, we'd eaten the entire thing," Marshall says with a giggle.

"Exactly how many pieces of my mail have you eaten?"

"Oh, lots," Marshall laughs.

"Remind me to install a new mailbox outside the house," I grumble. "I swear I never saw your special plan," I tell Ted. Even just saying those words creeps me out. This guy is so unbalanced.

"I don't understand," he says, scratching his head.

"You wouldn't believe me if I told you. So, you obviously had the right house."

"Of course! That's why I went to your house again on the morning of Halloween, hoping to discuss it with you, to help you see my side of things, but you weren't home. Even though your garage door was open, which isn't safe, I have to tell you. You should keep it closed when you aren't there."

No kidding.

"I was curious, so I went in to look around. When I saw a hatchet on the wall, it spoke to me, so I took it down. It felt so nice in my hands." He smiles like he's recalling a pleasant memory.

"Hang on a second. If it felt so nice in your hands, why weren't your fingerprints on it?" I'm not even pretending to be subtle now. I can't believe what I'm hearing.

"I was wearing gloves. It was a chilly morning, you know. I stared at it for a long time, and then it came to me. It was the answer to all my problems. I had to kill Herbert Appleton! But once I got home, I realized if I touched it without gloves, my fingerprints would be on it, so I didn't touch it again until I went to the cemetery."

"You didn't set out to frame me, then?"

"Oh no. Not in the beginning, anyway." He shrugs. "But obviously, I didn't want my fingerprints on the murder weapon. I could go to jail for that, you know!"

"You don't say," I mutter.

"Then I realized you were a suspect, so that took the attention off me." He nods vigorously." Why would I tell the police it was me if they were ready to blame you for it, right?"

"But you said you were one of my biggest fans," I protest.

"Oh, I was! Until you ignored my special plan. Then I decided you weren't very nice, so better for you to get blamed than me. I knew eventually they'd start over with new candidates, and hopefully, I could talk one of them into implementing my plan. You're a sneaky lady, though, aren't you?" he says, wagging his finger at me. "Now that you've tricked me into confessing, I'll be going."

In the meantime, he's been so busy reliving the day he killed Herb that he didn't notice the CPPD cars that pull up to the cafe. Several customers already sensed what was happening and quietly tiptoed out the door.

"You won't try to stop me, will you?" he leans forward asking in a whisper.

"Not at all," I assure him, shaking my head.

"Good girl. That way, no one else has to get hurt. I'll leave town as I planned, and no one will know the difference."

"Exactly!" I tell him. I'd laugh if I weren't so worried that he may have a weapon hidden on him. Clearly, Detective Thomas heard everything, and now the officers standing in the doorway to the cafe have as well.

I'm ready to cast a freezing spell on him if necessary. After Charles did that to me on Saturday, I looked it up in an old spell book from Gran and practiced all weekend. No one will get the jump on me like that again.

Thankfully, when Ted spins around and sees the police officers, all he does is snap his fingers in disappointment.

"Aw phooey!" he complains.

I breathe a huge sigh of relief when the officers cuff him and haul him away. That nagging feeling I had before is completely gone. Life in Crested Peaks can finally get back to normal. Whatever that is.

Chapter 18

I can't believe it's finally here. My election night party. While I gather with my friends and supporters in the cafe to wait for the returns, I swear I have bats flapping around in my stomach. Normal people have butterflies. I get bats.

The Elections Division was confused but relieved when I called them again first thing Monday morning to tell them to disregard the message I left on Friday about dropping out.

My heart fills with gratitude as I watch Serenity and Miranda in the corner, laughing and joking. They're a little pale, but they're good otherwise. Even though their doctors advised them to stay home and continue to rest, they said they wouldn't miss this for the world.

Damien and Aranya went all out on party food. There's enough here to feed an army. They designed three separate specialty cheese boards, mouth-watering empanadas using a recipe from Damien's grandmother, colorful spring rolls with peanut dipping sauce, and a whole host of other dishes I have yet to try.

The bats keep me from eating much of anything. Drew sprang for expensive champagne, which they won't let me drink until after I talk to the reporters. I wonder if it's bad luck to drink celebratory champagne before I've won anyway. *If* I win, that is.

Miranda enchanted a massive projection screen on the north wall so we can watch the returns. I thought it was really cool until I saw myself interviewed by a reporter on tv. Seeing myself looking three times my normal size was shocking. For starters, I'm never wearing that lipstick color again. Why didn't someone tell me it looked like that?

Poppy put bow ties on Marshall, Marcus, and Stumpy. They'd never let *me* do that! Bubbles is wearing a floral wreath on her chunky, square head. She's so adorable I want to squish her cheeks. I overheard the rabbits discussing plans to get the flowers from her head so they could eat them. The catch is they want to do it without getting dog drool on themselves.

The election results are supposed to start at 7 PM, but we expect a close race, so this could be a long night. When the first batch of returns appears, Herb is ahead by several points. Everyone in the cafe boos.

"This is it," I tell Drew. "This is the day I lose the mayoral race to a dead guy. Why did I ever think this was a good idea?"

"You wanted to make a difference," he reminds me, hugging me tight. "You wanted to make Crested Peaks a better place. You wanted to be a champion for the little guy. No matter what happens tonight, you did this for the right reasons, and that's what counts."

I stare into his emerald-green eyes and sigh. "I still think I'm an idiot."

"Don't count yourself out just yet," he laughs.

For the next two hours, the results go back and forth. First, Herb is ahead, then I'm ahead, then back to Herb. But by 9 PM, I pull way ahead and stay in the lead.

At 10 PM, Channel 9 News declares me the winner by a surprisingly large margin 56 - 44.

I'm so shocked I can't move. I stare at the screen open-mouthed while everyone mobs me. People hug me, pat me on the back, and shake my hand. When they call me Madam Mayor, I laugh because I don't know what else to say.

If I thought moving to Colorado and taking on a breakfast cafe was a giant leap, this is gargantuan in comparison. I just hope that I can live up to everyone's expectations.

"Can we lay off finding any dead bodies for a while?" I joke to the rabbits. "I have a feeling I'm about to get very busy with other things."

The rabbits just laugh.

Oh, dear.

More Books by B I Skinner

Ghostly Glenwood Mysteries Paranormal Cozy Mysteries

The Case of the Haunted Hotel

The Case of the Pilfering Poltergeist

The Case of the Poached Peridot

The Case of the Gym Ghost(Pre-order)

Spooky Shanty Realty Mysteries

Afterlife in the Attic(Pre-order)

Marcall's Breakfast Cafe Paranormal Cozy Mysteries

An Eggscellent Day for Murder

24 Carrot Caper

Daggers and Donuts

Cupcakes and Corpses

A Crime of Cranberry

Peppermints & Pandemonium

Star Spangled Homicide

Blood Curdling Ballots

Sign up for my email list here

https://mailchi.mp/9ebce0da866a/email-signup-list

Visit my website

biskinnerauthor.com

Follow me on Instagram **@bethiskinner** Facebook **@biskinner-author**

Copyright 2022 by Author B I Skinner. All rights reserved.

Cover art by B I Skinner

No part of this publication may be reproduced, distributed or transmitted in any form or by any means, including photocopying, recording, or other electronic or mechanical methods, without the prior written permission of the publisher, except in the case of brief quotations embodied in critical reviews and certain other noncommercial uses permitted by copyright law.

Note: This is a work of fiction. Names, characters, places, and incidents are a product of the author's imagination. Locales and public names are sometimes used for atmospheric purposes. Any resemblance to actual people, living or dead, or to businesses, companies, events, institutions, or locales is completely coincidental.